D1546101

INFINITE JES
by Sam Starbuck

3 1712 01606 2427

Copyright 2022
All rights reserved
Produced in the United States of America
First Edition

The text of this book is set in Garamond.

This novel is the eleventh volume published by
Extribulum Independent Press
extribulum.wordpress.com
Printer's Row, Chicago, IL

Nameless – 2009
Other People Can Smell You – 2009, Revised 2010
Charitable Getting – 2010
Dr. King's Lucky Book – 2011
Trace – 2011
By The Days – 2011
The Dead Isle – 2012
Six Harvests in Lea, Texas – 2020
The Found Fortune Deck – 2022
Fête for a King – 2022
Infinite Jes – 2022

ISBN 979-8-9859604-2-6

This book contains some material which may be triggering or upsetting, although generally brief. For a full list of content warnings and spoilers, please turn to the last page of the book.

CHAPTER ONE

"UNTIL A FEW months ago, not a lot of people knew about Askazer-Shivadlakia, the little country by the sea," Jes Deimos said, reading off a script but doing a good job of sounding like they weren't. "Maybe geography students with very niche grants, or historians interested in the effect of the Russian Revolution on European monarchy."

They paused, to audibly end the paragraph and also give the editor a little space to work with later if he needed it.

"But recently the country became a meme and a hot new Photogram destination – we'll get to that later – and suddenly it was everywhere. Even then, you might assume you've never *met* anyone from Askazer-Shivadlakia. You'd probably be right…unless of course you've been to one of my live shows. Because then you've met me!"

Noah leaned in towards his mic and said, "And me!"

"That's my son, Noah," Jes said.

"Hey everyone!" Noah added. Jes gave him a thumbs-up.

"I was born in Askazer-Shivadlakia, and Noah and I are both Shivadh. This season on *The Echo*, we're moving back to the Old Country, to see what's changed and to learn more about one of the only democratic monarchies in the world," Jes continued. "We've been back for family vacations, but never for very long. There are several reasons for that, all of which we'll be exploring along with the politics, history, culture, and daily life of our parentland. I'll be coming to you with weekly updates – "

" – and I'll be doing my own show for my listeners," Noah added.

1

"We're lining up guests as we speak, including one or two celebrities," Jes continued. "Join us in the echo, won't you?"

They held the silence until the recording light went off.

"Solid take," came the voice over the speaker, and Jes gave the tech a nod. "We're on a ten minute break."

"Thank you, ten minutes," Noah acknowledged. The tech grinned at him as he left. "How'd I sound?"

"You always sound perfect," Jes told him. Noah rolled his eyes. "You do! It's those youthful vocal cords. This is why, if I ever catch you smoking, you're both fired and grounded."

"Yeah, yeah," Noah replied, waving a hand. "Do you think they listen to the podcast in Askazer-Shivadlakia? I mean, aside from Nona and Granddad."

"Metrics say there's a small listenership. Probably mostly relatives, even after you take Nona and Granddad out of it. Not unusual for American podcasts," Jes said. "If I did true crime we'd maybe have a bigger audience and I wouldn't have to rob a bank to send you to college."

"Why go to college if you could rob banks?" Noah asked. "Bet people in Askazer-Shivadlakia will listen after you start posting episodes."

"I hope so. If I'm going to move back home, I can at least make a little trouble while I'm at it," Jes said. "Still okay with the move, kiddo? It's not easy to start fresh in the middle of high school."

"Not that hard," Noah mumbled. Jes felt a swell of sympathy for the kid. It was tough to be both smart and shy as a fifteen-year-old who was only famous on the internet.

"Well, it'll be an adventure. But if you get homesick or anything you tell me, okay? Family before business," Jes reminded him. "The podcast is never as important as you are, you know that."

"My podcast is way more important than you are, though," Noah told them, grin returning.

"The thanks I get for bearing and raising you," Jes scolded.

"Can I go get a snack from the vending machine?"

"Sure, here," Jes said, and passed him a couple of dollar bills. Noah bounced out of the room, and Jes sorted through the script folder, making sure they hadn't left anything out for today's recording session. The ad for the new season in Askazer-Shivadlakia should have been the last of it.

It might be rougher on Noah than he expected, Jes thought, but the kid was young and resilient. Jes wasn't sure how they themself would cope. It wasn't that they didn't like Askazer-Shivadlakia, but they'd been gone for ten solid years before ever going back, and even now they hadn't been back for more than a week since leaving –

Well, since running away, really.

But the world was changing, and there was a new king on the throne – a gay king, out and proud, and word through the queer and expat grapevines was that Askazer-Shivadlakia was a particularly friendly place to be right now. Lachlan needed them, and politically it wasn't a bad time to be moving back.

"Hope you know what you've gotten yourself into," Jes muttered.

It wasn't easy to travel incognito as a king, even the former king of a very small country.

Michaelis ben Jason, King Emeritus of Askazer-Shivadlakia, had developed a couple of techniques over the years. His son favored driving around in a battered truck and trusting the population to ignore him, which seemed to be working well, but Michaelis had loved spy novels as a child and enjoyed the occasional disguise. For many trips he'd worn a sort of subtle costume meant to imply he was either a tourist or a businessman; currently he had a goatee, which was doing a lot of the work, combined with a nondescript brown suit and a pair of spectacles.

It helped that his portrait on the currency was a few decades out of date at this point, but he tried not to think about what a great natural disguise crow's feet were.

The train between Paris and Askazer-Shivadlakia was a full-day trip, but that didn't matter to him; it wasn't like he had a busy schedule. He'd made the trip mainly as a favor to Simon, the royal family's personal chef, who needed some supplies most easily acquired there. Simon hated Paris for reasons Michaelis had never inquired about, and didn't like having to spend two days on a train round-trip and an overnight in the city, so Michaelis had volunteered.

It got him out into the world for a while, and he'd enjoyed himself – finished a book and started another on the trip up, shopped in Paris not just for Simon but also for himself, and had a good dinner in a nice outdoor cafe. He had a new book for the trip back, and when he got tired of the book, the train carriage was just busy enough to do some enjoyable people-watching.

They weren't that far from his stop when he noticed one of the other passengers, a dark-haired teenage boy in very American clothing, plastered to one of the windows a few rows up, craning his neck to see where they were going. His traveling companion, who Michaelis couldn't see much of over the edge of the seat, appeared to be asleep.

"If you're looking for the border marker, we passed it about ten minutes ago," he said, and the boy's head turned sharply, startled. Michaelis gave him a reassuring smile. "We're officially in Askazer-Shivadlakia now."

The boy scrambled out into the aisle, coming to Michaelis's row. He had a little bag with him, slung over one shoulder.

"Do you live here?" the boy asked, and if his clothes hadn't identified him as American, his accent would have.

"I do," Michaelis said. "I'm just coming back from Paris."

"We came through there from New York," the boy said. "I'm

Noah. I'm moving to Askazer-Shivadlakia."

He pronounced it with the casual cadence of someone who was used to saying the words, not like an American at all, and Michaelis tilted his head, interested. His eye caught the cord emerging from the bag Noah carried, and Noah saw him notice it. He opened it up to reveal a recording device of some kind.

"I'm a broadcast journalist and I make podcasts," the boy said hastily, running the words together like he'd rehearsed them but hadn't had a lot of opportunities to use them. "Can I interview you and record it?"

Michaelis raised both eyebrows. "You're very young to be a journalist."

"I know," Noah said with a grimace. Michaelis smiled.

"Certainly. Take a seat," he said, moving Simon's hamper to the floor. "I'm Mike."

"Thank you for letting me record," Noah said, pressing a button on the device in the bag. "Why are you going to Askazer-Shivadlakia? I mean going home, I guess."

"I was in Paris, picking up some things for a friend. What were you looking for? Was it the border?"

"Oh, no," Noah said. "I saw the border sign. I was looking for the synagogue."

"Ah!" Michaelis nodded. "Should come along soon – you'll know because the train blows a warning whistle when it crosses a main road just before it. You won't see it for long, but the view is superb."

"Have you been in it?"

"Oh yes – often, when I was younger. My father made sure we went every week. Not as much once I was grown and working – High Holy Days, mostly. Should go more often, to be honest, now that I can."

"What do you do?" Noah asked. "For work, I mean."

"I'm recently retired. I used to work in government. Very boring stuff," Michaelis assured him.

"What do you think of the new king?" the boy asked.

"Hard to know yet," Michaelis said, a little amused. "He's only been king for two months."

"But do you think he's going to do a good job?"

"I certainly hope so. He seems to be, so far." The train's whistle went. "There we go, here, switch with me..." He shuffled aside and let Noah take his window seat. The boy lifted his phone, camera app open, but Michaelis noted with approval that he leaned the phone on the sill of the train's window, so that he could record it but also watch the real thing pass by at the same time.

"There it is," Michaelis said, almost as excited as the kid was. The Grand Synagogue of Askaz was well worth watching for, even at speed from the train. It rose out of the flat landscape like a jeweled treasure box, sunlight glittering through dozens of stained-glass windows, ornate pomegranates crowning the corners, stone songbirds adorning the roof gutters. It was a long time since he'd seen it through a newcomer's eyes.

"Wow," Noah breathed.

"You should go and see it, if you can," Michaelis told him, once it was past and Noah had stopped the video recording. "They do tours, if you don't want to attend a service."

"We're going next Friday," Noah said. "Maybe. Soon, anyway. What else do you think I should do in Askazer-Shivadlakia?"

Michaelis could hear a certain tone in the boy's voice that said this was a Proper Interview Question, but he'd been interviewed by many older, stupider people asking much less interesting questions.

"Well, the palace is architecturally very interesting, and the grounds are at their peak right now, in the spring and summer," he said. "The conservation officers teach bowfishing lessons on the lake, but you'd probably have to get permission from a parent for that. There's a little art museum in town, and I know the king's been thinking of building a science museum. I suppose there's not a lot for a boy your age, though," he added, frowning. "No... amusement parks or malls or whatnot. We do have very good internet, though."

"What do you like to do?" Noah asked.

"Oh, be outdoors, I suppose," Michaelis replied. "Never got to do as much of that as I liked when I was working. Hiking, fishing, swimming."

Just then, the train's conductor came over the loudspeaker – "Fons-Askaz, next stop Fons-Askaz in three minutes!"

"That's my stop," Michaelis said.

"Mine too! I did some reading, it means – "

"Caesar's Fountain, yes," Michaelis said, amused.

"Noah?" a voice called, and Noah looked up only a little guiltily. Whoever he was traveling with was moving around now, gathering up bags from beneath the seats.

"You'd better go get ready," Michaelis added.

"Thanks for the interview. Here," Noah said, and gave Michaelis an actual business card. He hadn't been handed a business card in probably a decade – it was all digital now, or so he'd thought. "If you want to hear the podcast you can listen there. Maybe I'll see you in town!"

"Maybe," Michaelis agreed, tucking the business card in his pocket. "Very nice to meet you, Noah."

The boy shook his hand and dashed back down the aisle; Michaelis heard him call, "I'm here, I was just doing some recording."

He would have gotten up and introduced himself, but just then the conductor announced they were arriving at the station. In the bustle of getting himself and his luggage off, and dodging around other people trying to do likewise, Michaelis lost sight of the boy and his guardian. Then staff were there to collect him up into a car, and he was being whisked back to the palace.

"Simon!" he called when they arrived, leaving the driver to take his bag, carrying the hamper into the kitchen himself.

"Your Grace!" Simon replied, hurrying up to take the hamper out of his hands. "Thank you. Oh, beautiful," he added, popping the lid up to look inside, examining the cloth-wrapped cheeses, the packets of herbs, and the steel kitchen implements he'd asked for. "Exceptional."

"Happy to be of service," Michaelis replied. Behind Simon, he could see Eddie, Gregory's boyfriend, pulling something out of the oven. "Pizza again, Edward?"

"Hot slices ready in five," Eddie confirmed, sliding the pizza onto a nearby board. "Welcome back, Your Grace. Have fun in Paris?"

"I did, actually, thank you. I'm in time for dinner, then."

"Sure. Greg's not even down yet. Running late because of some kind of argument about tariffs. Not sure what tariffs are, but I'm strongly against them in general, for his sake."

"Import-export fee, essentially," Michaelis replied. "I'm sure he'll be along soon."

"Go on ahead into the dining room. This has to stand first and I need plates," Eddie said. Michaelis gave him a nod and headed for the small dining room nearby, where the king and his close family generally took their meals. The king was, as Eddie had warned, not in evidence, but his cousin and assistant Alanna was, so he probably wouldn't be too late. Jerry – Gerald, 12th Duke of Shivadlakia and technically the king's vizier, an honorific bestowed mainly as a joke – was also there, working on a Sudoku puzzle.

"Welcome back," Alanna said, as Michaelis pulled out a chair. "Shopping go well?"

"Paris was delightful. Usually is," Michaelis agreed. "A nice change of scenery."

"Eiffel Tower still standing?" Jerry asked.

"I didn't inspect it personally, but it seems fine," Michaelis replied. "What new trouble have you got into while I was gone?"

"None at all, I've been very well behaved."

"Mm, you must be feeling ill."

Jerry pretended to be wounded, then got distracted when Eddie arrived with the pizza on a tray in one hand and a stack of plates in the other.

"If you're tired of pizza, Simon said to tell you he also has soup and sandwiches," Eddie announced, "but this is a new crust to keep things interesting."

He presented a slice to Michaelis first, then to Jerry because otherwise he'd have had to fend him off with the serving spatula. Alanna, either more patient or just not as eager for pizza, took hers with more dignity.

"Which iteration is this, Eddie?" she asked, tearing off a piece of crust to sample it.

"Ah, this is Eddie's Perfect Pizza Pie test version 4.2," Eddie said, seating himself and setting out two more slices, one for himself and one for Gregory. "Malt crust, more sugar in the sauce, surprise cheese."

Michaelis, who had been dissecting the slice in front of him with a fork, looked up curiously. "*Surprise* cheese?" he asked.

Eddie gestured at Jerry, who was already halfway through his slice. "It's just Provel. I thought the cheese needed a little more grease. Promise I didn't poison it."

"No point now, I'm reduced to harmlessness already," Michaelis said, breaking off a small chunk with his fork and tasting it. "Decent," he pronounced.

"I don't think you could ever be harmless, Uncle Mike," Jerry said.

"Well, politically," Michaelis said. "I'm getting extremely good with a bow, even off the water. Thinking of going on a boar hunt in the autumn. That's a very elder king thing to do and Edward's keen, aren't you?" he asked Eddie.

"Anytime you want. I'll carry your bags and make sausage after," Eddie agreed.

"Seems a shame to go to all the trouble for something Uncle

Mike won't eat," Jerry said.

"I'll eat them," Alanna said, smiling at Eddie.

"I'm in it for the hunt, Gerald," Michaelis replied. "You don't eat pork sausage either, don't talk to me about sausage."

"If I never hear about sausage again, frankly, I'll have lived a full life," a voice announced, as Gregory arrived in the dining room. He bent to kiss Eddie hello, then settled in next to Michaelis with a nod. "Welcome back. Nothing against boar sausage in theory but it's another damn luxury export. We could've been the Geneva Freeport, but no, we chose ethics and cured meats instead of catering to the richest men in the world."

"I warned you," Jerry said. "A moral stance is an invitation to ruin."

"Jerry, what you said was *you can't get in trouble if they can't catch you*," Gregory replied. "Malt crust?" he asked Eddie, who nodded.

"The spirit was there," Jerry said. "Anyway, your dad and Eddie are planning their own deaths."

"Boar hunt," Eddie explained.

Gregory nodded. "Yearning to have a folk song written about you, I remember."

"Because His Grace was just grumbling about harmlessness," Alanna said, and something in her tone made every man in the room look at her.

"Do you take issue with my grumbling?" Michaelis asked, genuinely surprised. Alanna was a sweet girl; not a truly malicious bone in her body, which meant this was about something else.

Alanna and Gregory exchanged a look. Michaelis gestured back and forth between them. "What's this conspiracy? You've already got the throne, there's no point murdering me now."

"Alanna – and Eddie too, to be fair – has mentioned to me that you...talk a lot about how useless you think you've become," Gregory said. "It's become a little worrying, I think."

"It's just small talk," Michaelis said.

"Is it?" Gregory asked. "I know handing off governance

wasn't easy."

Michaelis glanced from Alanna to Eddie, and then at Jerry, who gave him a shrug.

"I wasn't in on the conspiracy," Jerry said.

"Nice to know I have one ally, even if it's only because he's clueless," Michaelis said.

"That's fair," Jerry agreed.

"Dad, this isn't a coup, you don't have allies and enemies," Gregory said, rolling his eyes. "Nobody's staging an intervention. Just making sure you're all right."

"I'm fine," Michaelis said. "A little bored, but I'll adjust. That's what retirement is. You have to complain about it before you settle in. Probably why your grandfather disappeared for months after my coronation."

"Well, so long as you know we're here for you," Gregory said.

"The royal family's only allowed two emotions per year," Jerry said to Eddie, who nodded. "I always feel so privileged to see it."

"All right, let's let it go," Gregory said. "Alanna, what am I doing tomorrow, aside from slowly losing my mind at the damn EU?"

Michaelis leaned back, letting the conversation wash past him, full of palace operations he was no longer a part of. Jerry scooted a little closer.

"Offer stands, Uncle Mike," he said. "I could get you a reality show in no time flat. Call it *The Retirement Plan*."

"*Old Idiot Yelling*," Michaelis replied.

"I mean, that probably has great SEO."

"What on earth is an SEO?" Michaelis asked.

"Search Engine Optimization? Means you're easy to find when someone searches you."

"Easier to find than I already was as king of Askazer-Shivadlakia?" Michaelis asked, raising an eyebrow.

"...you've got me there," Jerry admitted.

"Thank you for the offer, Gerald, but I'm not quite that desperate yet," Michaelis said.

"Your loss," Jerry said. That was the nice thing about Jerry: he might be a troublemaker at times but he was generally low-maintenance, one-on-one.

Michaelis poured himself a glass of the wine that Eddie had paired with the pizza, frowning when the flavors didn't quite mesh. Eddie raised an eyebrow at him and gestured at the wine; Michaelis nodded and Eddie made a note in his phone. Maybe he ought to spend more time with the man; they'd gotten off to a slightly rough start, but Eddie was settling in nicely. And he was good for Gregory, very obviously so.

On the other hand, Eddie then began Photogramming his new pizza, and Michaelis was still very wary of social media. Maybe wait a while longer. Plenty of time to plan that boar hunt.

"Who were you talking to, anyway?" Jes asked, disembarking from the train that evening. They kept an eye out for their parents, but the platform was crowded with people coming and going. Fons-Askaz wasn't as quiet and sleepy as it used to be, they thought.

"Just a guy coming back from a trip, I guess," Noah replied. "He was showing me how to tell when the synagogue is coming."

"Oh, when the whistle blows! Yeah," Jes said. "You were careful?"

"I'm always careful," Noah said, affronted.

"Yes, but you are also a wild child who talks to strangers."

"I am a journalist," Noah informed them. "I was recording."

"And someday I'm sure your recording will be evidence in the kidnapping case," Jes said, ruffling his hair. He batted them away. "You're taller than me now, tell me when you see Nona and

Granddad."

A shriek split the air, and Noah's head jerked around; he blurted "Uncle Lachlan!" and took off running. Jes stayed where they were, hobbled by the luggage, as Noah threw himself into the arms of a tall man with wild hair and multiple tattoos – including a few that looked new since the last time they'd seen him.

"JES!" Lachlan yelled. "HE'S TOO BIG!"

"I keep saying," Jes said, as Lachlan dragged Noah back to where they were waiting. They accepted a hug from him and then he turned to hug Noah again, ruffling his hair.

"Look at you, honey," he said to Noah. "So tall and so ready to break hearts! If you want to. If you don't want to, that's valid, and you could break laws instead."

Noah grinned at him. "Not ace so far, but I'll let you know."

"And not in prison for lawbreaking either. Shame. Well, notify me if I need to buy a new flag at any point. Your parents were parking the car last time I saw them," Lachlan told Jes. "I'll take you there. *I'll take you there,*" he sang the last part again, in a soulful voice. "*Ain't nobody cryin'...*"

"Come on, Uncle Lachlan, that's the Staples Singers," Noah said. "Give me a challenge."

"Later, princess. My charm offensive against your Nona continues, and she doesn't like singing in public."

"Lord," Jes sighed.

"Deep breaths. It's only temporary until you find your own place. I've been fixing up the studio, too! All the equipment's in, but I was waiting for Noah to help set it up."

"Thank you," Noah sing-songed.

"Sure thing. How was your trip? Everything go smoothly?"

"Noah made friends," Jes said. "He's getting a jumpstart on the podcast already."

"I got a list of some stuff to see from a guy on the train," Noah said.

"Well, once you're moved in and recovered from the jet lag,

we'll get the sound stuff set up and Jes can entertain themself while I take you touring. And Great Auntie Carla has ordered you to come to Friday night dinner," he added, including them both with a look.

"See, we've already got a social calendar and dinner plans," Jes said. "Thanks for coming, Lachlan."

"Of course. Couldn't wait to see you," Lachlan said, planting a kiss on the shaved side of their head. "Chin up, shoulders straight. You only need to be home six hours a night to sleep."

"It's not that bad," Jes said.

"We'll find you somewhere permanent to stay fast," Lachlan assured them.

Jes squeezed his hand, grateful for the support, and waved back when they saw their father waving from the car.

CHAPTER TWO

MICHAELIS HAD BEGUN to loathe his weekly visits to the library, which in itself was upsetting. Ordinarily he loved the library, but now he was visiting to dictate his memoirs to the royal librarian, and it was an exercise in frustration for them both.

Still, he'd scheduled his trip to Paris to interfere with the last one and he'd missed a further two already, so he really did have to attend this one. Even if it was just as difficult as the previous ones had been.

The problem, he supposed, as he left the librarian's office after yet another terrible hour, was that it was difficult to talk about some of the more sensitive political topics, and equally difficult every time he mentioned Miranda. But it wasn't as though he could ignore her in his history – she had been a vital presence on the throne, sometimes better at ruling than he was in those early years. And he didn't want to ignore her. He wanted her memory preserved.

He stopped near the big library doors, gathering his dignity and calming himself. He did what he'd found useful since her death, and pictured himself collecting up all the little pebbles of memory from that day, picturing them cradled in his palms. Mentally, he carried them to a cavern deep in his mind and set them there, near the entrance, smoothing them over until they were indistinguishable from all the others he'd left. Then he walked backwards away from them, until he could open his eyes.

He felt better already – calmer, more ready for whatever might confront him when he left the library.

He emptied his pockets onto the study desk next to him, just to make sure all his notes were in order. Tucked into one of them was a square of stiff cardstock – the business card that Noah from the train had given him.

NOAH DEIMOS
AUDIO ENGINEER - PODCAST HOST
HE/HIM

He took his phone out as he descended from the library to the ground floor, tapping in the website address from the card. There was one of those automatic feeds from Photogram, and he was startled to see footage from the train ride. He waited until he was outside to push play, and when he turned up the volume he could even hear himself say "There it is," excitedly, and Noah's soft "Wow," before the video ended. It reminded him of trips with Gregory and Miranda, sightseeing in between diplomatic stops and trade negotiations.

The website also had a link to a pair of podcasts – *The Echo* and *The Echo Junior*. He added them to the little widget that played the podcasts (Jerry hated it when he spoke about them that way, which was half the reason to do it) and took his headphones out of his pocket.

The walk from the palace to the fishing lodge wasn't long, and once you got used to the scenery it also wasn't that interesting. A good opportunity to see what the kid was about. He tapped open *The Echo Junior*, because Noah's name was attached to that one. The latest episode was called "Teaser Trailer: Season Five" and was only two minutes long, so he skipped it and went to an earlier one titled "Am I The Product?"

It was an interesting discussion, to be sure, about who profited from social media and who provided the content. Even without knowing much about the subject matter he could tell it wasn't a deep dive – it was made by and meant for youth. Still, that was helpful in its own way. Noah and his guests spent a lot of time explaining how social media worked on a basic level, which was quite educational. Michaelis mainly knew of Photogram as a tool the palace used sparingly and something Eddie had used to upend the entire country without even trying. Probably for the best that Eddie now worked for the palace and was taking a more measured approach.

He let the episode play through as he arrived at the fishing lodge and let himself in. It was really too big for one person, but staying full-time at the palace held less appeal for him right now. Besides, one didn't need to fill space just because it was there. He listened to another episode as he changed out of his suit and made a cup of tea.

The third episode had a different host, and when he checked his phone, it said this was *The Echo*, hosted by someone named Jes Deimos, apparently a relative. He paused it – plenty of time to encounter the grown-up version of Noah's podcast later – and instead switched over to some music before bed.

Still, the events of the day bothered him. He knew a historical record of the reign was important – he'd consulted other records himself – but the librarian had Michaelis's official diaries, and the whole point of being king was that if you did it right, nothing especially interesting ever happened. Interesting was the enemy of good rule. Still, the process shouldn't be boring, for him or for the staff, and it was. It was *astonishingly* dull. Michaelis was growing to dislike himself for how uninteresting he was managing to be.

The coolest he'd probably been in years was on the train from Paris, he thought. Showing off the synagogue, advising a newcomer on what to see and do in his home.

He picked up the business card again, studying it, and noticed there was also an address printed on it. Reverb Podcast Network's studio was located in Fons-Askaz, the harbor town below the palace – right on the main street, not even that far away. A podcast studio in Askazer-Shivadlakia seemed like a very modern thing to have, and probably quite interesting.

He sat on the bed, considering this. Obviously the kid was too young to help, but surely someone at the studio was responsible for him, and that person probably knew how to conduct an interview that wouldn't make him seem like a droning old bore. Jerry had suggested a reality show –

Gregory had also suggested a podcast. Months ago, and mostly in jest, but…it had a certain appeal. His speeches had usually gone over well, in no small part because of his voice, and as soon as he'd worked that out he'd made sure to preserve it. Miranda used to say he sounded like a bass drum wrapped in velvet, which had always made him preen a little.

Well, no harm in asking. And it would probably please Gregory, who clearly was fretting (unnecessarily!) about his mental state.

Resolved, he laid out casual clothes for the following day, mapped the location of the Reverb Podcast Network's studio on his phone, and went to bed.

The recording studio, if he had the address right, was in a small block of offices at one end of the high street. He wasn't in a particular hurry and the weather was clear and warm, so he walked into Fons-Askaz at a leisurely pace, with the wide town harbor on his left and the palace up the hill on his right, until he got down far enough that the palace receded into the distance.

The building was old and didn't look well-kept. When he let himself into the main entrance he found a grubby, quiet hallway inside. Third door down was the studio and the handwritten hours card taped to the door said it had been open for an hour, so he turned the handle and peered inside, a little wary.

It opened into a small waiting room with a few seats and two tables, one of which was near a window looking out on the harbor. That one was occupied –

"Noah!" Michaelis said, startled. He hadn't expected the boy to actually be here. The dark head of hair at the table looked up, and Noah beamed.

"It's Mike, right?" he asked, bouncing to his feet. "What are you doing here? Did you look up my podcast?"

"Yes, in a way," Michaelis said, coming into the waiting room and letting the door close softly behind him. A light over another doorway indicated someone was recording, somewhere. "That's how I found this place. Are you making a podcast today?"

"No, not today," Noah said. "Babysitting some guests for the other podcast."

"Right, *The Echo*," Michaelis nodded. "You do the Junior version – I listened to a few episodes."

"Oh cool! Is that why you're here? I'm definitely going to put you in an episode, but it won't be out for a while," Noah said. "I could do another interview if you thought of more stuff to see."

"I wouldn't mind, but I'm here to speak to whoever owns the studio," Michaelis replied. "I've been thinking of doing a podcast myself."

Noah blinked at him. "About Askazer-Shivadlakia?"

"Maybe indirectly. If I promise I won't steal your thunder, can you introduce me?" he asked.

Noah was opening his mouth to reply when several things happened at once.

The recording light over the door went out and the door itself opened. A handful of people emerged, more or less filling the little space. One of them said, startled, "Your Majesty!"

"Esta?" he asked, surprised to find an MP in a podcast office – although Esta Jerome had been a junior MP during his reign before advancing and was still very young, so perhaps he shouldn't be.

"Noah?" one of the other people said, and Michaelis squinted past Esta, trying to determine if he recognized them. After a second he realized he couldn't even place their gender, let alone their face.

They were fairly short, with curved hips and a flat chest, what he'd have called a feminine face with a strong jawline. Their bleach-white hair was combed into a pompadour on top of their head, the sides shaved. They looked older, closer to his age, but dressed like one of Gregory's fashionable school friends, in a tailored shirt and a kilt in purple and black.

"Uh, Boss, this is Mike, the guy I interviewed on the train," Noah said.

Esta said, "Mike?" in an intensely amused voice. The man next to her gasped dramatically.

Michaelis tried to stop gaping at everything happening around him and summoned forty years of dignity as a king.

"I was just speaking with Noah about his podcast project," he said.

"Noah," the other person said, going to the boy. There was an unmistakable family resemblance – the same narrow face and snub nose, dark heavy brows and pale eyes, but this one had the Shivadh accent, if a little faded. "Did this man introduce himself properly to you?"

"I'm afraid I was incognito when we met," Michaelis answered. He gave Noah a brief nod of a bow. "Michaelis ben Jason, King Emeritus, at your service, young man."

Noah stared at him. His – mother? Parent? Boss? – nudged him gently. It occurred to him this was probably Jes Deimos, though that was not especially helpful.

"Nice to meet you," Noah said. "Again."

"Esta, thanks for the interview," the person who was probably Jes Deimos continued. "Lachlan, can you walk her out?"

"Can I come back and eavesdrop after?" the man called Lachlan asked. He looked like he was savoring this.

"No," the person said.

"Fine. Bye, Noah, be good," Lachlan said, and then it was Michaelis, Noah, and this mystery person.

"I go through this a lot," Michaelis said, "but I think you have the advantage of me."

"Jes Deimos," they said. "I'm Noah's parent."

"I gathered. I'm sorry, the boy did nothing wrong – he didn't know who I was when we spoke," Michaelis said.

"Boss, he said he wanted to talk to the owner of the studio," Noah said. "About um. Doing a podcast."

Jes Deimos' face managed to combine "amused" and "deeply unimpressed" in a way that was pure Shivadh.

"Are you the studio's owner?" he asked, still trying to cover his surprise. "I was under the impression Noah had just moved here."

"I'm a partner," they replied. "You want to do a podcast?"

"Yes. Well. I'd like to ask about them. I really know very little, but I listen to some, and they seem…popular," he said.

"Normal mid-life crises usually involve a shiny car, not a recording studio," they said.

"I'm afraid I'm a few years past mid-life and I already have a shiny car," he replied evenly. To his surprise, they laughed.

"Well, all right, we're a public studio and we do offer our services. I assume you have all the funding you need. Have you lined up any marketing or advertisers?" they asked, heading for the door in the other wall. "Step into my office."

"I only came up with the idea yesterday," he said. He held the office door for Noah, looking back; the boy seemed surprised, then followed them in.

Jes's office was a small cubby lined in noise-dampening foam, with a large glass window looking in on a recording studio. He suspected it might double as a second studio at times.

"So, tell me why the former king of Askazer-Shivadlakia wants to do a podcast," they said, sitting down at the desk, gesturing him into another seat.

"Traditionally, if a king retires rather than dying on the throne, one of his emeritus duties is to dictate his memoirs to the royal librarian," Michaelis said. "It's considered an important historical record. Kings have often consulted the previous memoirs for precedent. Even after the monarchy became democratic and our needs, in terms of advice, were different."

"Ish," Jes said.

"Beg pardon?"

"Democratic-ish. After all, your son is the third generation in your family to be elected."

Michaelis shrugged. "My son and I both won fair elections against strong candidates, which is more than can be said of some American political dynasties. Why, are you bucking for the job?"

Jes laughed again, seemingly startled by the retort.

"That's fair," they agreed. "Your memoirs aren't a full explanation, though."

"No, I suppose not. I've been doing my best, but it's very tedious," he said. "And, as a former king, one does feel useless. I didn't want to keep on in international politics, and Gregory has the country well in hand. I suppose I'm searching for a challenge. A podcast seemed like a chance to learn a new skill, perhaps improve my storytelling. I'm afraid most stories involving my reign are not very interesting, but I don't need to be a sensation."

Jes studied him, which was a little unsettling, but the entire encounter so far had been. He glanced at Noah, who looked excited.

"I'm going to act self-interestedly here," Jes said finally. "Because it's not every day a former monarch walks into my office and wants to hire my services. But I think it would also be genuinely useful to you to see how podcasts are made before you decide you want to make one. They're more work than they seem, and most podcasters don't get past the seventh or eighth episode."

"Good lord," he said.

"So I'd like to invite you onto my podcast," Jes continued.

"*The Echo*?" Michaelis guessed. Noah snickered.

"The same. You can follow me through an entire episode,

from idea to finished product, and if you think you're still interested at the end, we can discuss next steps."

"Boss," Noah said. Jes looked at him. "Dibs."

Jes threw their hands up in the air and sat back, groaning, a reaction that surprised him; Noah grinned and pointed at them.

"Fine. Noah did get you first," Jes told Michaelis. "Technically I'm inviting you onto his podcast, *Echo Junior.*"

"Or we could do a collab," Noah said. "We make a podcast about making a podcast. You can be the point of view, like we teach you how to make it," he said to Michaelis. "Then if you want to make your own, you can."

Jes had seemed irritated by Noah's dibs, but now they looked at Noah like...well, the way he'd looked when Gregory was taking his first wobbly steps into politics.

"I think that sounds like a fine plan," he said to Noah. "How do we begin?"

"We have a brainstorming meeting on Tuesday," Jes said. "You can come to that. How do I put something on the calendar of the former king of Askazer-Shivadlakia?"

Michaelis spotted a little pile of business cards on the desk, and picked one up; it said, on the front

JES DEIMOS
BROADCAST JOURNALIST - AUDIO PRODUCER
THEY/THEM

Well, perhaps that explained a few things. He turned it over, took a pen from the cup on the desk, and wrote out his email address, passing it to them.

"This is your personal email," they said, studying it. "Not the palace one that goes to a screener."

"Yes?" he replied, perplexed.

"You don't use a secretary?"

Michaelis shook his head. "There's not much call for my

services, as I said. Anyone who wants me for official business goes through the palace. For personal concerns, the email suffices."

"Well, I will have my secretary send you an invite," Jes said, passing the card to Noah, who got out his phone and immediately started tapping away on it.

"Can I ask," Michaelis said, standing to leave, "why Esta Jerome was here?"

"Nervous about an MP speaking to a journalist?" Jes asked, standing also.

"I think you overestimate the level of power I wield or the amount of control I want," Michaelis said. "I like Esta; she's sensible and she's a great supporter of the king's initiatives. She's destined for high office if she keeps on the way she's going."

"I'm sure she'll be glad to know it. She's a friend, and she's in local politics, so I wanted to interview her, that's all."

"I look forward to hearing the interview," he said, as Jes held the door for him. "I'll see myself out. Until Tuesday. Noah, good to see you again."

"Your Majesty," Noah said, and Jes elbowed him. Michaelis smiled and let himself out into the hall. He had just stepped into the sunlight outside when his phone buzzed and an invitation to *Echo/Jr Weekly Brainstorming* appeared on the lock screen. He accepted it and pocketed the phone again.

Well, a radio journalist of indefinite gender and a kid who wasn't afraid to commandeer the former king of his country into a podcast scheme. If nothing else, life was certainly looking more interesting, at least as far as next Tuesday went.

As soon as the former king was gone, Jes slumped against the wall outside their office and slid down it until they plopped on their ass on the floor.

"Wow," Noah said, because Noah was their child and

therefore a little bit of an asshole sometimes. "You really had the sass turned up high. Did he kick you when you were a kid or something?"

"Shh, I'm decompressing," Jes replied, and Noah sat down next to them. "Only you."

"Me? How is this my fault?"

"Only you would make friends, randomly, with the king of your native homeland!" Jes said. "I didn't expect a former monarch to walk in today. I would have put more product in my hair."

"Your hair looks fine."

"That's missing the point, but I suppose that's my fault too, probably," Jes groaned. "And now he wants us to teach him how to do a podcast. I'm going to have to show the king how to run a soundboard."

"You taught me."

"Your brain is young and elastic, love," Jes said, pulling Noah into their side.

"He is kinda old."

"Watch it. He's not that much older than me."

"He seems like he learns stuff. You know how some people just never learn stuff. He looks like that's not him," Noah said, considering it. "If he was king for all that time he must've been pretty good at keeping up."

"You'd be surprised what politicians can get away with, especially when they're pretty. But you may be right. I suppose we'll find out," Jes said. Their phone buzzed and they checked it. "Ah. Lachlan wants to know if the coast is clear and he can come back in to scream with us about what just happened. Would you go get him? I need a minute of silence to rethink my life choices."

"Yeah, I got it," Noah said, getting to his feet and heading for the door. A minute later, Lachlan could be heard making a series of high-pitched enthusiastic screams, growing ever closer. Jes got up and dusted themself off.

"Oh my *shit*, that was the ex-king," Lachlan cackled, throwing himself through the door, down the hall, and into their office. Jes followed more calmly. Noah, wisely, went back to his work in the waiting room. "He is hot in person. That steel gray hair? And legs for days. *And* that voice. Bet he can purr like a cat. What did he want?"

"Podcast advice," Jes said.

"He could read the dictionary and we could sell it. Did you give him your number?"

"I think he took a card," Jes answered, frowning.

"Did you give him my number?"

"Lachlan, I love you, and you are a beautiful person inside and out, but the former king, who was married to the same woman for his entire reign and lost her tragically to illness less than a decade ago, is never going to sleep with you."

"He might be bi. Anyway, the royals demonstrably have no taste in men. His son is dating Eddie Rambler."

"Even if he is bi, he doesn't seem the type for casual sex."

"I'd marry him if it was required, I'm not doing anything more interesting," Lachlan said, putting his feet up on the desk.

"Your husband and infant child might take issue."

"They'd recover. By the way, did you see him check you out?"

"I saw him visibly trying to figure out what pronouns to use. Thankfully the business card was a hint. Hopefully he picked up on it."

"I think he liked your hair. Good thing you wore the kilt today."

"I'm sure he's seen nicer knees. Did you want something?"

"Other than another three days minimum spent drooling over King Michaelis? Not particularly. Let's go have an early lunch with cocktails."

"Lachlan, seriously," Jes said. "Don't tell the world about this, okay? I don't need that kind of publicity and I'm sure he doesn't. He sounded like it took a lot for him to come here."

Lachlan sobered, folding his hands over his stomach. "Of course, Jes. Promise. Nobody hears it from me."

"And if you behave yourself, you can come sit in when we do the tech stuff, maybe show him how to check his levels."

Lachlan waggled his eyebrows. "I'll be the soul of discretion."

"I'm sure you will. Anyway," Jes continued, pushing his feet off the desk. "Let's go over scheduling. The number of people who want studio space is kind of shocking, to be honest."

Michaelis was at breakfast in the palace on Friday, which surprised Gregory when he walked in. Usually, if he was planning to stay at the palace over the weekend, he didn't show up until dinner time.

"Might just be you and me for breakfast," he said, helping himself to a scone from the basket on the table. "Alanna took Jerry to do some errands, and it's Eddie's slow day so he was still asleep when I left. How's the lodge?"

"Still standing," his father replied with a smile. "I came up to see you, actually."

"Well, you know I always like to see you around the place. Anything in particular we needed to discuss?"

"Nothing official. I was thinking of going to Kabbalat Shabbos tonight at the Grand Synagogue, and wondered if you wanted to come."

"Oh, that sounds nice," Gregory said thoughtfully. "And I should go more often. Kingly thing to do, now that life has settled down. Any particular reason?"

"Not really," his father said, in exactly the tone of voice that would once have made his mother suspicious of ulterior motives. She would have asked him about it, and Michaelis often did need to be prodded a little about his thoughts. But Gregory had always felt when his father was being devious, adventure was in the wind. He didn't need to know the precise nature of it.

"Well, I'm in, doesn't look like I have anything on my calendar," he said, consulting his phone. "All right if I invite Eddie? He probably won't come, but he likes to be invited to things."

"No objections. Meet at the staircase? I can drive us."

"Sure. Are you in the palace today?"

"No, just came up to see you. Need anything from me?"

"Actually, if you can put your head in at Parliament briefly, Sorensen is still treating me like I'm a stand-in until you get back. Can you be boring about fishing at him for half an hour?"

"Love nothing better," Michaelis said. "There's a man who desperately needs to retire but his district simply won't stop electing him. Irritating him is always a pleasure."

"I'm seeing to the issue. There's a junior MP who could replace him handily, they just need a bit of help strategically. Alanna's hatching something."

"Very good." Michaelis grinned at him. "Now, tell me what you think of this news out of Italy last week…"

It was the best spirits Gregory had seen him in for some time, and after breakfast he enjoyed watching his father take one of his most irritating MPs down a peg. Perhaps the fishing lodge was doing him good, instead of the harm Gregory and his cousins had worried about.

It used to be that a Shivadh king, arriving to any service at the Grand Synagogue, would basically take over the show – received in splendor, seated in honor, and generally distracting from what should have been religious observance. Michaelis had read several historical accounts in the library by rabbis who'd been very angry about it. But that was one of the many changes Gregory II, his son's namesake, had introduced. He'd stopped attending any religious observance entirely, and then when he began again it was subtly, quietly. It was tradition by now, several generations strong, that the kings of Askazer-Shivadlakia basically slunk in the back like tardy schoolchildren.

Michaelis liked it. They arrived about five minutes late, both in the sober black uniform of the royal family, and slipped in through a side door, held open silently for them by an usher. There was a bench in the back specifically for the royal family, and he settled himself next to Gregory on it. The air inside was pleasantly cool, but the light was a deep warm orange, sunset streaming in through the big windows from the west while indigo night was falling in the east. And this had always been his favorite service to attend, between the singing and the murmured prayers. Welcoming Shabbos and a late dinner after, that was a good evening in his mind.

He didn't know if Jes Deimos and their son would be attending, but Noah had said they planned to at some point. He wouldn't admit to something as blasphemous as going to synagogue just to see someone he was curious about, but it was high time he got back here, as Noah's questions about how often he went had proved.

It was good, anyway. He could feel his shoulders dropping, and Gregory seemed to be relaxing too.

He did spot that knot of white hair, very visible in any crowd – Jes Deimos, about halfway up in the congregation, Noah a lanky shadow next to them. Noah looked like he was having more fun than his parent was. A pair of older people next to them, probably Noah's grandparents, seemed happy enough to be there. The man he'd seen at the studio, Lachlan, was behind them, and occasionally squeezed Jes's shoulder.

And of course, someone took Michaelis's picture.

He didn't notice at the time, but it didn't take long for the photo to get out. He wasn't even asleep that night, in his rooms in the palace, when Gregory knocked on his door.

"I don't think this is an emergency," he said, "but it's very funny and also something you should know."

He switched on the television in Michaelis's living room and held his phone up, pairing them. His phone's screen appeared on the TV, showing a picture of him and Gregory, in their matching uniforms and their kippahs with the royal crest, sitting attentively on the royal bench. It had been posted to Photogram, with the caption *Kings greeting the Shabbos Queen. You love to see it.*

"Is that a Shivadh Photogram?" he asked. "Not an influencer or someone, I mean." Gregory nodded. "Hm. Bad form to be taking pictures in shul, but I suppose at least they had good intentions. Decent photo, too."

Gregory tapped a button and a very, very long string of comments unfolded.

"Oh dear," Michaelis said.

"It's mostly positive, at least about us," Gregory said. "Some people agree with you they shouldn't have done it."

The first comment, upvoted the most, was *I didn't think old Mikey'd been back since Queen Miranda passed. Good for him.*

"If I was offended every time someone called me that I'd have quit the job thirty-nine years earlier than I did," Michaelis said, as Gregory scrolled. "Anyway, they aren't wrong. It's been years. My own fault."

Another comment near the top was *Pair of deadass foxes.*

"That's a compliment, isn't it?" Michaelis asked.

"Yes. There are roughly fifteen separate comments calling you a silver fox," Gregory said, amused.

"Again, I've been called worse. What are they calling you?"

"Well, one person said I was a Shivadh snack, which is about the most absurd. The most upvoted compliment was that I'm short, dark, and handsome, which made Eddie laugh. There's not a lot of real ugliness, and half of Askazer-Shivadlakia downvotes it whenever it pops up, so it's essentially invisible the second it appears."

"Mm, and it's not like we didn't get all that before," Michaelis agreed.

That's cool and all but isn't it kind of super disrespectful to Jews? someone had written. *Shouldn't you be invited before you go to services?*

Michaelis opened his mouth but Gregory said, "Wait for it," and opened the comments thread below.

Found the American gentile, the first comment said.

Imagine having to be invited to the synagogue you were married at, the second one added.

Harold, they're Jewish, the third one said. Michaelis cracked up laughing.

"I recognize that joke, Edward taught me that meme!" he said. "You're right, this is funny."

"Now that the country's the center of social media attention, it might go on like this for a while," Gregory said, disconnecting from the television. "I'll get briefings from comms regularly, but I was wondering if you wanted to know when you show up on social media."

"Do you think it's necessary?"

"I don't know yet. It's all new to me, too. Generally it's been kinder to us than the tabloids, but it can get vicious and there's no editor to stop it when it does. Nobody to sue, either."

"Hm." Michaelis crossed his arms, considering. "I don't really need the flattery. I made it a point never to read my own reviews unless they had genuine impact on the governance of the country. That said, I do want to know if something's brewing that you or I will need to manage. Can't have myself turned into a meme every time I go for a walk. What does Edward think?"

"Eddie's an influencer," Gregory said. "He manages his spin himself, and he's much better at it than we'd be."

"Then I think I should ask him to keep an eye on my hashtag, or whatever they're using to identify these things, and if he sees something I should know about, he can tell me."

Gregory was biting his lip. Michaelis raised an eyebrow.

"Eddie said the exact same thing. He's the one who found this one," he said, wiggling his phone. "Says he's happy to do it but wasn't sure you wanted him to."

"As long as it doesn't waste his time," Michaelis replied. "He's technically palace staff now, he shouldn't be made to overwork."

"Oh, believe me, nobody has to make Eddie overwork," Gregory replied. "I didn't realize we were *both* fifteen-hour-day kind of people."

"This brings up a point," Michaelis said, because he'd been turning it over in his mind since seeing Deimos earlier. "Did you know there's a person in Fons-Askaz making a podcast about the country?"

"What?" Gregory asked.

"I don't have much information about it yet. An expat moving back from America. They say they're going to do a series about Shivadh culture, the country...probably your rule. They've already spoken with Esta Jerome."

"Can you send me what you have?" Gregory asked, brow furrowing. "Copy palace comms, perhaps?"

"It didn't seem malicious, for what it's worth," Michaelis said. "Esta wouldn't stab you in the back."

"No, but this is still the kind of thing one has to keep an eye on. I'll speak to Esta about it."

"I wouldn't do that yet," Michaelis said. "Just...I'll send you what I have in the morning, you can look it over then."

"You're sure?" Gregory asked. Michaelis pulled him in by the back of the neck, kissing his forehead, a reassuring gesture since Gregory's childhood.

"Trust me. This doesn't have to get resolved tonight. I'm keeping an eye on it too. Remember, it's Shabbos. At least take the night. Go spend some time with Edward. Get some sleep."

"Fine. It's a good idea," Gregory said with a smile, conceding. "Sleep well, Father."

"You too," Michaelis said, and when Gregory was gone he settled into the couch to read for a while, pleased with the world despite the presence of Photogram in it. It was, actually, a little nice to be in the public eye again, and one did like to hear every once in a while how handsome one was.

CHAPTER THREE

MICHAELIS SPENT THE weekend at the palace, mostly puttering around. He went running in the mornings, worked on the massive project of putting forty years of his papers in order, and played football with the weekend staff, though his knees protested later. On Sunday, he spent the afternoon with Gregory in the kitchen, tasting various dishes Eddie and Simon were concocting. He'd always liked the royal kitchen and Gregory had loved it from childhood, so it wasn't exactly a trial.

Whenever he could, he had his headphones in, and Jes Deimos's voice in his ear.

He knew Gregory was listening as well, and both of them had plenty of reason; if a prominent journalist was going to do an entire series about the country, they ought to know as much as possible. Palace comms wasn't thrilled, but Gregory didn't seem overly worried after he listened to the trailer and a few of the earlier episodes.

And *The Echo* was fun to listen to, purely for entertainment – Michaelis could see why it was popular. Deimos was never aggressive, exactly, but they had a way of pulling a person apart with exacting slowness to get at the meat of what they had to say. He'd have to watch himself a little around them, but that could be fun, too.

They did human-interest pieces and political reporting; an entire season dedicated to the lives of students at a New York performing arts school, and one where they did nothing but interview people the listenership had nominated as thought leaders of the day. They did retrospectives on old news stories that had apparently revolutionized how people saw certain historical events, and they had a running, years-long series on sexuality and gender identity that Michaelis probably could have used when Gregory was coming out, and Gregory definitely could have. They chronicled almost the entirety of their friend Lachlan's marriage, from his third date with his now-husband to the day they adopted their child. They did an episode about what it meant to identify as butch, followed by one about what it meant to come out as nonbinary, to explore genderqueer identities. There seemed to be a lot of discussion and disagreement about the vocabulary, but even that was an education.

He didn't always listen to all of an episode, or every episode in a season, but that was sort of the brilliance of podcasts, he thought; you could just jump around as you pleased, most of the time. He kept a list of other shows they recommended, and his player filled up so fast he had to slim it back down again. Most of the voices were American, but not all, and the more he listened, especially in the evenings when his time was hard to fill, the more intrigued he became. By Monday night, when he was settled back in the lodge with a glass of wine and *The Echo*'s first episode about Askazer-Shivadlakia, he was looking forward to the brainstorming meeting the following day. And he was secretly a little pleased that he was *in* that first episode, taken from Noah's recording.

At Mike's request, Deimos said, voice rich with amusement, *though we have some more information about what he recommends to see and do, we're holding off on sharing it for now. You'll be hearing from him again!*

Tuesday dawned stormy, an unexpected summer rain drumming on the tin roof of the lodge by the time Michaelis woke, so he exercised rare royal privilege and called up to the palace to ask someone to drive down with his car. Normally the trail from the lodge to the palace was a nice morning stroll, but he wanted to look like a genteel retired royal rather than a drowned rat.

And he asked for the Jaguar.

Well, Deimos's remarks about mid-life crises had stung a

little, and on the off-chance they caught him pulling up, the sight of the bottle-green Jag he'd been given for his fiftieth birthday would be amusing.

When he arrived at the studio, Jes and Noah actually were outside, but not for any good reason he could see. Noah had his arms full of equipment wrapped in plastic, and Jes was escorting him hurriedly to a van already full of the stuff, a huge umbrella in one hand. He parked the Jaguar behind the van and climbed out, pulling his coat's hood up to keep the rain off his head.

"What's going on?" he called through the downpour.

"Leaks!" Jes yelled back. "Meeting's canceled!"

"How bad a leak?" he asked, baffled by this, and then looked at the office building, which had water pouring out of the front door. "What in the…"

"Kinda bad!" Jes said, as Noah thrust the equipment into the van's open door.

"Let me help," he said, running through the streams filling the front walkway, up to the building's entrance. Inside there was an inch of water in the waiting room of the office. He darted back out into the hall, dodging drips and streams, and lunged for the fuse box he'd seen earlier, pulling it open and flicking all the electricity off.

"What're you doing?" Jes demanded, coming inside. They kept the umbrella up, but Noah ran past them both into the darkened office.

"Turning off the electrics. If the water reaches the outlets and they're live, we'll all die very unhappily," he said, switching on the flashlight on his phone to illuminate the hall. "How can I help?"

"We've got most of the delicate stuff out. It's just furniture and one of the heavier pieces of equipment," they replied. Noah was clattering around in the studio, from the sound of it. "I didn't know this place was made of cardboard when we rented it."

"It does seem to be worryingly disintegrating," Michaelis said, looking around. "Who else is in the building?"

"As far as I know, nobody. At the time I thought that was great, less noise, but now I'm thinking this is probably why we got it cheap. Dammit," they growled, running fingers through their wet, disordered hair. It dripped onto the baggy sweatshirt they were wearing, creating a constellation of darker dots on the already damp grey fabric over the NYU logo. They sloshed forward, Michaelis following. "Noah?"

"I can't get the board on my own!" Noah yelled.

"Here, let me," Michaelis said, slogging to where Noah was trying to wrestle something flat, wide, and enormous off the table. "If you cover us with the umbrella, we can get this out together," he added to Jes.

"I don't think there's room in the van for it and me," Noah said. "If we can get the board in the front seat you can drive it back, and I'll wait here."

"Not indoors, this is a death trap," Jes said. Michaelis, hefting one end of the board, eyed it speculatively.

"I've got a car," he said.

"You've got a Hot Wheels. It won't fit in the back seat you don't have," Jes said.

"So put it in the van. I'll take Noah and follow you to wherever you're taking it all," he replied.

"Shit, I don't even know. My parents' garage, maybe. They're going to love that," Jes sighed. "But it's dry, at least. Mostly."

"Let's get it out of here," Noah urged.

They managed to haul it out to the van and load it into the front seat, upright, belted in like a passenger, then huddled under the umbrella to confer.

"That's the last of it," Noah said. "Unless you want to – "

He was cut off by an almighty crash; behind them, part of the roof of the building caved in. The family Deimos stared at it.

"You know," Michaelis said, "I think I'm going to have a word with our municipal government about building inspectors picking up the slack a little. We have safety laws in this country."

"That'd be helpful, yes," Jes said. "What a disaster."

"At least you're out, and this looks like very difficult equipment to replace," Michaelis observed. Thunder crashed. "We should get inside. Look," he added, because both of them seemed miserable and he was starting to really feel how wet his socks and shoes were. "There's a cafe down the block that's probably structurally sound. Let's take a break and dry off. I'll buy you a coffee."

They looked more bewildered than anything, and he understood the feeling, so he hustled both of them down the sidewalk and into the cafe, where other equally-wet people were drying out. A few of them looked his way and whispered to each other when they walked in, but Michaelis settled Jes and Noah at a table and then went to the counter, where the barista at least knew him slightly and wasn't entirely bowled over by him walking into her cafe.

"Your Grace," she said. "You look like you've been through it."

"There has been," Michaelis told her, "something of an incident. Could I lean on your patriotic spirit for a couple of dishtowels?"

"I know their regular orders," she said, nodding at Jes and Noah. "Yours plus theirs?"

"Please," he answered, swiping his card as she rang him up.

"No charge for the towels," she said, handing him a stack from under the counter. "I'll call when the drinks are up."

He carried the towels back to the table, using one to dry his face and passing the others to Jes and Noah. Jes seemed glad to be able to put their hair in order, and Noah was mostly dry once he'd patted all the rainwater he could off his legs.

"Well, you aren't seeing us at our most professional," Jes said, through the towel, "but you are, I have to say, seeing us at our most resourceful."

"I've found professionalism to be vastly overrated,

generally," he replied. "Glad I could help."

"Thank you," Noah said, poking his parent with a finger.

"Yes, we do appreciate it," Jes added, giving Noah a look. "Can we pay you for the coffees?"

"Consider it a down payment on my podcasting lessons. Though I don't think you'll be back in that particular studio anytime soon," he said.

"We've got two weeks' worth of shows in the can," Noah said to Jes, who looked annoyed and disconsolate. "I can do some extra-fast editing once we record and if we can get a new studio set up we won't really miss much time."

"Should you not be in school?" Michaelis asked, realizing it was early May and the schools generally didn't let out until June.

"He's enrolling in the fall. By the time we got set up here, he'd have three weeks left, so we decided not to bother," Jes said. "Didn't seem worth it to send him to school just for exams." They gave him a challenging look. "Going to narc, Your Grace?"

"Beneath the notice of a king," Michaelis answered, amused. "No, it's not my business, and he seems like he's learning something, anyway."

"I could be doing that project on fundraising you wanted me to do," Noah said to Jes. "If you let me take some pictures in the studio I can – "

"You can't go back in there," Michaelis interrupted, appalled. "It's not safe. The whole damn thing looks like it's going to slide into the harbor."

"I'm light," Noah said to him with a grin.

"Allow me to introduce you to the wild child," Jes sighed. "He's right, Noah. We'll shoot some of you looking sad and wet next to the van. Hah! We can call it Noah and the Flood."

Noah made a waifish, pathetic face. Michaelis smiled.

"What do you need the funds for?" he asked. "I would hope it was insured."

"We were renting. Even if the building is insured the money

mostly won't come to us, and our business insurance is going to take an eternity to pay out. We've got to rent a new space, which means new deposits and costs. We'll have to get it all set up again, and replace at least two of the mics well before insurance pays, if it ever does. We put up the soundproofing ourselves, so we'll have to either buy more or wait to salvage what's in there. It's…doable, but not great," Jes said. "We're living with my parents right now. We were planning to find a place and move out, but we can use the rent budget if we have to."

The barista called "Deimos!" and Noah got up to go get the drinks. Michaelis rested his chin in his hand, considering. There were arts grants available and he was sure he could divert grant money for this, but it would look like personal use, given he wanted to use the equipment as well. But…the fishing lodge was technically state property, and it had plenty of empty space. Damn thing was built like a bunker – in fact, the basement had been expanded into one –

"That's very imposing," Jes said, and he looked up from his thoughts.

"What?"

"The face. You look like you're bored at the UN," they said, gesturing to his face as Noah set a coffee in front of him.

"I'm sorry, I was just thinking," he said. "I'm staying at the fishing lodge right now, out on the palace grounds. The basement was built out as a bunker during the war. It's already pretty soundproof. You only need my permission to use it, which I'm more than willing to give. And there'd be no charge."

"Ah," Noah said, and they both looked at him. "Can I record this?"

Michaelis grinned at him. "Want a second take?"

"He's already recording on that damn pocket mic, he's just asking for permission now," Jes accused. Noah flushed. "Noah!"

"It's fine, I expected no less from a *broadcast journalist*," Michaelis said, gently teasing. "It really is, I don't mind," he repeated to Jes, who didn't look entirely appeased. "I suppose if you're making a podcast about Askazer-Shivadlakia this is probably very good material."

"You're still supposed to ask before you start recording," Jes said. "That's basic ethics."

"Can we get back to the bunker?" Noah asked. "I want to record in a bunker!"

"It seems as though your day has been pretty much wiped clean of meetings," Michaelis pointed out. "At least come and see if it would be useful to you. If not, we can always take the equipment to your parents'."

Jes nodded. "All right, we might as well take a look. One of us is going to have to ride with you in the Hot Wheels, though."

Half an hour saw them running through rain that had only slightly lessened; Noah, leggy and with the energy of youth, outdistanced them both and got into the van. Jes yelled, "Noah!" in a frustrated tone that Michaelis remembered from when Gregory was a teenager: annoyance and resignation rolled together, that their fifteen-year-old had made a unilateral decision they didn't agree with.

"Get in out of the rain before you yell at him," he said, holding the door on the Jaguar for Jes, who looked askance at him but climbed in. He circled around and got behind the wheel, shaking water off his hands and arms.

"He knows he's supposed to ask first, and only drive the van on side roads," Jes said.

"He's fifteen. You let him drive it at all?"

"Well, sixteen is the legal driving age in the US, you know," they replied. "Sometimes when it's just you and your thirteen-year-old kid and you have to get recording equipment somewhere, you have to improvise."

"*Thirteen?*"

"This is why I can't punish him too badly for it, I created him," Jes said, as their phone beeped. Michaelis could see the single word text from Noah: *Dibs...?*

"It's not far to the lodge, and mostly on a back road," he offered. Well, Gregory had been captain of the shooting team at school when he was fifteen, and giving a child a rifle was arguably a worse idea than putting them behind the wheel of a car.

"*Fine,*" Jes said, typing out a message back. "*Next time ask.* And, send," they said. "You'll have to drive ahead, to show him where to – oh, no," they said, as he started the car.

"What?" he asked.

"This is the shiny car, isn't it. You drove your midlife crisis car here just to tweak me?"

He shot them a smile and pulled out of the parking space, gesturing for Noah to follow him.

The disintegrating recording studio was relatively close to the turnoff for the back entrance to the palace grounds; it didn't take them too long to pull onto the bumpy road to the fishing lodge. In deference to the equipment he drove slowly so Noah, apparently a cautious would-be driver, could follow at a sedate pace. Normally he would have pulled around to the front of the lodge, but there was a loading dock down into the bunker, so instead he guided the Jaguar down the ramp and into the covered underground garage.

"Well, this is...definitely...concrete," Jes remarked, getting out. Noah bounced out of the van and looked around eagerly.

"Is this the bunker?" he asked.

"Through here," Michaelis said, leading them deeper into the dimly-lit garage and through the thick entry door. Inside, he took off his drenched shoes and wet socks, and saw the others following suit.

The bunker had been renovated from a simple cellar into a long-term shelter, and the previous royal family had lived there for a period during the war. It had a series of empty bedrooms at the back, a little kitchen off to one side, and a large central room that had served as a war room of sorts, with an extremely yellowed and outdated map of Europe still on one wall. A smaller room off to the side had been a playroom and nursery for the royal children once; beyond that was a network of corridors connecting different parts of the bunker to each other, old walled-off boltholes, supply closets, and the garage. It would have been unpleasant to live in, and some of the rooms were now simply storage, but it was well-lit and well-ventilated, and quiet.

"We could put up like four studios in here!" Noah called from one of the former bedrooms. "The soundproofing's already great! Little bit of foam, run some extension cords…this'll work!"

"As you can see, it's also watertight," Michaelis drawled. Jes cracked a smile as they examined the ancient cookware still on the shelves in the kitchen.

"I can't object to the rent," they said. "And Noah approves, so we can work with it. I never knew this was here. I mean, the fishing lodge, we did field trips as kids, but they didn't show us the bunker."

"Shame. It's very historic – they ought to start showing it on tours. But it's also not very useful, empty like this," Michaelis said.

"You're living here?"

"Upstairs in the lodge proper. It's a little nicer," he said.

"Why not at the palace?"

Michaelis shifted uncomfortably, looking away. "Well, the whole point of retirement was that I could spend more time fishing," he joked, but Jes didn't laugh. "Beats trying to rule a country."

"Well, if that's your yardstick, life's a breeze," they said. "Noah?"

"Yeah!" Noah emerged from the back, looking around interestedly. "This is super punk rock," he declared. "It's awesome, we could definitely fix it up."

"There's parking and space," Jes agreed, looking around. "Are you sure we won't disturb you?"

"Separate entrance, and concrete ceilings. I probably won't

even notice you're here," Michaelis said. "During daylight hours you'll have lake access, too. The conservation officers don't love strangers out on the grounds at night, but the view at night's a little lacking anyway."

Noah had his phone out and was already taking selfies.

"Come on, kid, let's get the equipment loaded in," Jes said, casually putting their child in a headlock and dragging him away. Michaelis followed and was promptly tasked with fetching and carrying, since he had no clue how anything should be set up. He brought most of the equipment in, while Noah set it up and Jes settled into a dusty chair to inspect each piece and do any triage for later repair. By the time Noah said they were set, it was past noon.

"Come upstairs," Michaelis said. "Have lunch before you go."

"Coffee and lunch? The generosity of the king knows no bounds," Jes said, following him up the stairs.

"Former king," he corrected with a smile, elbowing the door to the main lodge open.

Jes had to admit, when they'd arrived at the studio that morning to find it falling apart, they hadn't expected to be eating lunch in a warm, dry bungalow with the former king.

Noah, the bottomless pit, was plowing his way through an entire bag of potato chips, which didn't seem to bother Michaelis, who had set out makings for sandwiches and left them to their own devices while he took down plates and cups. The lodge was large, meant for entertaining, and it wasn't difficult to tell how little space Michaelis took up – the kitchen was tidy but lived-in, and there were newspapers folded up next to the nook in the kitchen where he clearly ate his meals. The formal dining room and ballroom that they remembered from childhood field trips were closed off, but the living room that the kitchen opened into had blankets on the sofa, books strewn around, and a jigsaw puzzle on the table in the corner.

"This kitchen is huge," Noah said, settled at the dining table in the corner. "I think our whole apartment in New York'd fit into it."

"Used to be two," Michaelis said. "The old kings were more observant – needed the separate kitchens. My father had it converted to the one big one, put in the bar between the kitchen and the living room, did a few other renovations. He had to have the whole building rewired – before it couldn't even support the one refrigerator, always blew fuses when I was a child. Really should replace that fridge," he added. "The renovation was mostly to make it easier on the caterers when we entertained out here. It's pretty big for one person, but I suppose if I ever wanted to throw a dinner party I'd be glad of it."

"And it's just you? I suppose I assumed you'd have a chef and a couple of maids," Jes said, settling in next to Noah.

"I could, but I didn't see the point. I'm not what you'd call an inspired cook, but I can shift for myself, and Gregory would miss our chef, Simon, if I took him away. Not to mention he'd be incredibly bored just cooking for me," Michaelis replied. "It keeps me busy."

"Do you have to keep it pretty neat?" Noah asked. "If it's historic, I mean."

"Usually nobody's living here long-term, and there aren't any school tours left this term," Michaelis answered. "In any case, I'm a fairly tidy man. Gregory's the messy one. Don't put that in any podcasts," he added, pointing at the recorder sitting out on the table. "Can't have the king mad at me."

Noah made a careful note on his phone, checking the timestamp on the recorder.

"Well, you are all business, aren't you?" Michaelis asked. "Suppose you've been apprenticing for a while."

45

"Is that what I'm doing?" Noah asked Jes.

"You can call it that if you want. I kind of like the ring of it," Jes replied. "Noah Deimos, apprentice podcaster."

"Shame you already had the business cards printed," Michaelis said.

"Oh, no, the business cards..." Noah looked at Jes in alarm. "They were in the office."

"Well, then it's a chance to print some new ones," Jes told him. "They have the wrong address on them now anyway. I'm sure we're going to spend the next week thinking of things that were in that office. Probably for the best we hadn't decorated."

"At least this way we won't lose much time," Noah said. "We could be up and recording again this afternoon if we wanted. Can we offer studio space to the people who wanted to rent some?" he asked Michaelis bluntly.

"We'll have to invoice for equipment and time – can't charge for the space itself," Jes said. "Might actually bring our prices down, which could bring in more artists. Don't mind that."

"Well, it sounds like you know what you're doing. Just keep them from wandering. I'll get you a set of keys for the garage entrance," Michaelis replied, more agreeably than Jes might have, if it meant strangers were going to be in their basement all day. "Convenient for me, I must say."

"Ah, his true motives are revealed," Jes said to Noah. "See, you're getting good at this interview thing."

"I'm known to be nefarious," Michaelis said. "I promise I won't be a nuisance, though."

"Why's it so crazy down there, anyhow?" Noah asked. "Walls a foot thick, weird hallways going off to nowhere."

"The fishing lodge dates back a couple of centuries," Michaelis said. "You'd probably have to look in some archive, somewhere, but what I've heard from various sources is that it originally just had that single big room, essentially a cellar. It was used as a shelter during the First World War, but it wasn't really *designed* as one. Then Gregory II – "

"The one who made it a democracy," Noah said.

"It's like the single fact about this place he knows," Jes told Michaelis.

"More than some know," Michaelis replied. "Gregory II had it reinforced after the war, and about fifteen years later when he saw what was going on next door, he decided to expand it into a space they could live in. Hide in. If they had to."

"Hide from what?" Noah said.

Michaelis fixed him with a level gaze. "Who would we have been worried about, in 1935?"

Noah's eyes widened. "Nazis?"

"Italy's on our doorstep. Germany's not that far away," Michaelis said. "Gregory II was an unusually farsighted ruler. He anticipated a lot of 20th century history. Askazer-Shivadlakia basically emptied out in the 1930s – he sent as many people away from Europe as he could. Our own private little diaspora within a diaspora."

"And the royal family hid here?"

"For a time. We – the country, I mean – were incredibly lucky. Not many roads or rails in or out of the country, nothing at the time that would support a tank, and we could booby-trap the lowlands and the harbor. We had some foreign support from the Allies, too, though it's not entirely clear as to how. We made it just slightly too painful for anyone to bother with us. We're of no strategic importance and we were surrounded by enemies. So I think," he said, taking a sip of water, "that more than one army looked at this little country and said, *we'll deal with you later.*"

"But they never did," Noah said.

"No, the Americans came up through Italy first. We gave them a good beach-head. There were some Shivadh soldiers among them, actually, there's a memorial in town. We didn't get out of the war without harm, but…" he shrugged. "We survived. We're the only Jewish monarchy in Europe. Which Gregory is discovering has its own issues," he added.

"See, this is good material," Noah said. "Boss, there's maybe a history episode in it."

"Perhaps," Jes said. "Maybe Michaelis wants to be the one to tell that, though."

"Don't know. Always a little dicey, bringing it up," Michaelis said. "Some ugly conspiracy theories are attached. I'd want to make sure I had all the facts first."

"How would you see your podcast working, anyway?" Jes asked. "Like one story a week? Formal interviews? Do you want to get the royal librarian involved?"

"Couldn't say. I hardly know what I'm doing, which admittedly is a feeling I haven't had in a while," Michaelis said. "I've been listening to yours, though. And a few others. I don't think I care for those shows where it's just one person talking. That's really nothing more than a book on tape, eh? No disrespect to them, but a conversation – like the shows you do – that's much more interesting and I'll need all the help I can get."

"But you did spend forty years deep in European politics," Jes said. "I know Askazer-Shivadlakia used to host diplomatic talks as a neutral ground. You were king when the Berlin Wall fell."

"I wasn't king of Germany," Michaelis pointed out.

"No, but it must have had ramifications for you. Hang on, this is Noah's job," Jes said. "Let's step back a little. You don't like your storytelling, that's what we should tackle first."

They looked at Noah, who considered it. Michaelis waited patiently, working his way through half a sandwich.

"Can you tell us one of your memoir stories?" Noah said at last. "As if you were dictating to us. Like, show me what's boring you, I guess. Don't tell a boring story, just tell a story," he added, seeing Michaelis's expression. "And then we can help you."

Michaelis sat back for a minute, finishing his bite of food, took a sip of water, and thought about it.

"Well, I left off with some trade negotiations about six months before Gregory was born," he said, and launched into a story that was so unbearably boring that Jes was actually shocked.

Watching such a charismatic man suddenly lose his entire persona was baffling. Two minutes into it they looked to Noah, who seemed equally surprised. Three minutes in, Michaelis stopped of his own accord and spread his hands.

"You see the problem," he said, with a self-deprecating smile.

"At least you're aware of it," Jes said. "That was extremely boring, but I've been bored by professionals who didn't even know they were doing it."

"It's mostly 'cause it's about something boring, I think," Noah said.

"It's important, though," Michaelis replied. "This kind of detail. It's the kind of thing I used to look up in the indices when I was a new king, so that I'd know what to do. Maybe it's better written down," he added. "Not good fodder for a show."

"You do have to pick and choose, with audio media," Jes agreed. "An interview format would probably be more helpful. Or, maybe not an interview exactly, but something structured. We can workshop it. There's plenty of time, anyway, it's not like you have a deadline."

"Why didn't you ask your dad?" Noah asked. Michaelis frowned.

"Ask him what?"

"Why didn't you ask him stuff instead of looking it up? He was still alive, right?"

"It's complicated," Michaelis said. "The simplest way to put it is that I wanted to prove I could rule without him looking over my shoulder. And also the second I was crowned he left the country on an eight-month goodwill cruise."

"Nice work if you can get it," Jes said.

"He wrestled control of the country from an incompetent tyrant and affirmed democratic rule of law. I feel like he earned it," Michaelis replied.

"This is already way more interesting than the trade negotiations," Noah said to Jes.

"Good, then you're on the right track," they replied.

"My opinion on my father's round the world cruise isn't really relevant, though," Michaelis pointed out.

"I suppose you'll need to decide if you want to be educational or interesting," Jes said. "It's an ongoing tension in this business."

"Wouldn't one ideally want to be both?" Michaelis asked.

"Sure, but you can't be both one hundred percent. And fifty-fifty doesn't always satisfy either."

"Nobody likes a compromise," Michaelis murmured, almost to himself.

"You're a politician," Noah said, like he was reasoning something out. Michaelis nodded. "So it's like writing a speech, isn't it? You have to share information but keep people interested. Did you have to learn to do that? Or was it, like, natural?"

"I had rhetoric and oration at school," Michaelis said. "But you do learn as you go, in my line of work."

"Then you can learn this too!" Noah said brightly. "It'll just take practice."

"I appreciate the encouragement," Michaelis said. Jes caught the faint hint of amusement, but they could tell Noah hadn't, nor was he meant to.

"We've monopolized you for long enough today," they said, gathering up the remains of their lunch to dispose of it. "Noah and I should really see about talking to the landlord."

"I'll get you a key to the bunker – come and go as you like," he replied, ducking out of the room. "Back in just a minute."

"Do not sass him more and ruin this for me," Noah hissed when he was gone.

"I haven't sassed!" Jes replied. "What am I ruining?"

"A super cool concrete bunker in the middle of a literal forest I didn't know was here!"

"It's the palace grounds. It's a public park."

"Still. This place is great and free and probably has secret passages and hidden rooms," Noah said.

"There is a missing wine cellar," Michaelis replied, coming back into the kitchen, a set of keys in one hand. He passed them to Jes. "Somewhere under the lodge. Supposedly, anyway. Let me know if you find it."

"Thank you, again," Jes said, as Noah got ready to go. "This is really generous."

"Public property," he reminded them. "Your taxes at work."

"Well, I'll make good use of it, then," Jes said. "We'll reschedule the brainstorming meeting and send you an invite. Good day, Your Grace," they added, with a hint of sass just to tease Noah, and left the former king to the rest of his lunch.

CHAPTER FOUR

TIME BEGAN TO pass surprisingly quickly after that. Michaelis often dropped into the bunker in the mornings just to make sure Jes and Noah didn't need anything. They sometimes came up at his invitation to have a meal in the lodge, especially now that he had meetings with them to discuss the podcasts. Eventually Noah took to popping in and out at random, since it was easier to go through the lodge to get to the lake than it was to circle around from the bunker. Michaelis suspected on occasion it was also easier to rummage for snacks in the lodge pantry than go into town for them, but a stray granola bar or sandwich wouldn't break the royal pension.

Michaelis found his days much busier, and felt like he got out into town more; he went back to Friday night service, too. He knew Jes saw him there, but they didn't mention it, so he didn't either. Noah had homework for him on how podcasts worked, and he did some research of his own as well.

Eddie had taken Michaelis's request to hear about anything relevant to him rather liberally, and began sending him memes. Every few days he'd send a link to a Photogram post or video, or simply a photo someone had taken of Michaelis and captioned amusingly; apparently there was somewhere called r/shivadhkings that followed him and Gregory religiously. It was all rather flattering; if any of the comments were cruel, Eddie thoughtfully wasn't sharing those, or was dealing with them through the palace comms team.

Two weeks after the Great Flood, as Jes called it on their latest episode of *The Echo*, he came downstairs in the morning to a serious discussion, Noah's voice a little panicked, Jes sounding not entirely confident either.

" – won't be the worst thing in the world if we have to stay with Nona and Granddad until autumn," Jes was saying, as he walked in.

"Won't be great either, though," Noah replied. "You hate being there, and I guess I get why now. Even in New York we could always find somewhere."

"It's different here – it's a beach town. As soon as it gets warm, everywhere fills up, and it got warm super early this year. Even if there are places to rent, they're rented by tourists, and it's worse this year. Granddad's had offers on my bedroom that have made me seriously consider sharing with a random tourist."

"Why is it so bad?"

"Tourism's up. Eddie Rambler made it the place to be. Which we will definitely cover in our *Why Are We A Meme* episode," Jes said, and then saw Michaelis in the doorway. "Hey! Come in, we were about to get started reviewing the script for your first episode with Noah."

"Still looking for a place?" Michaelis asked, as he went to the kitchen, where a carafe of coffee was still steaming. "Every apartment in town can't be rented."

"No, but those that aren't are either expensive or about as durable as the studio was," Jes replied.

"I had a meeting with Alanna about that," Michaelis said, stirring sugar into the coffee. "She's going to push it to Parliament – new housing, maybe subsidized housing, and definitely more stringent building codes. A lot of the older buildings are from before my time and were exempt from previous changes in the law. Gregory will make sure things are put in motion. I wish I could say whoever built that mess could be beheaded but I'm afraid we did away with summary execution."

Jes laughed. "It's good of you to even have the king take an interest."

"Well, that's what he's there for." Michaelis sipped his coffee, considering. "In general the palace has been in support of Edward's, ah, enthusiasm about Askazer-Shivadlakia, but we certainly weren't prepared for how it would impact infrastructure. I don't think anyone in the world is truly prepared for Eddie Rambler."

"What's he like?" Noah asked. "He seems cool."

"He's very engaging. Surprisingly, also a good cook. Most of these TV chefs aren't, I have a feeling." Michaelis came to the table, settling in and accepting a tablet with his script on it from Jes.

"I saw a rumor on the internet that Edward isn't his real name," Noah said.

"And do you have an opinion about rumors on the internet?" Michaelis asked mildly. Noah grinned.

"Mostly lies, and only sometimes fun ones," he said. "Why do you suppose he'd do it? Change his name, I mean."

"Well, show business," Jes said. "People sometimes have to change their names for whatever reason. Anyway, I did," they added.

"I suppose I could have changed mine when I became king – some kings of Askazer-Shivadlakia did, way back in the past," Michaelis said thoughtfully. "That would have been too strange for me, though. Gregory thought about it, but only when he was a teenager."

"What did the rumor say Rambler's real name was?" Jes asked.

"Didn't, but they said they bet it had to be rough to change it to Eddie Rambler," Noah said.

"He does have a way of disturbing things," Michaelis said. "Such as, unfortunately, the housing market."

"Should see if we can move in with him," Jes joked to Noah. "It's fine, we'll find a place. If not now, then when the season's over, after the olive harvest."

"You'd be welcome here," Michaelis heard himself say, without even thinking about it first. They both looked at him. "The lodge, I mean."

"Down here?" Jes asked.

"No, that would be unbearably grim. There's space upstairs. You've seen the only working kitchen, but there's an otherwise self-contained suite you could use. Two bedrooms, sitting room, bathroom – I'm in the single bedroom suite at the back, but the two-bed is what we used to use when I was king, and it's serviceable. Or you could each have your own, but those are in the upstairs wing which gets quite warm in the summer."

Noah looked to Jes, who was studying Michaelis with an expression he couldn't quite discern. He hoped, more or less, that they weren't seeing right through his poker face, to how much the silence of the lodge sometimes troubled him.

"We can't live here *and* work here for free," they finally said. Michaelis smiled faintly.

"Technically there's probably some kind of grant you could get to be an artist in residence, so you could be getting paid to live and work here, but I see your point," he said. "Shivadh pride, you know," he added to Noah. "If you like, fix yourself a fair rent and make out a check to the steward of the palace; he'll know what to do with it. I'll get you his name."

Jes looked away, and he could tell his remark about pride had touched a nerve. "I'll think about it."

"Offer stands, no deadline," he replied, and sipped his coffee again. "Now, let's go over this script."

The next morning, Michaelis came out to find Noah in the lodge's kitchen, not the bunker, peering into a cupboard.

"I keep the crown jewels in the fridge," he said, and Noah laughed. "What are you looking for?"

"Coffee?"

"Ah, here," Michaelis said, taking it down from a different cupboard. "Guess this means you and Jes are moving in?"

"Yep." Noah sounded a little strained about it, so Michaelis let him make the coffee while he took down mugs and got cream from the fridge. "Nona and Granddad weren't pleased. They wanted me and Boss to stay there forever. Big fight, even though Boss only said we were considering the offer. I think the grandparents are going to sulk for a while."

"I'm sorry to hear that. Gregory wasn't pleased when I moved out here, but at least he understood."

"Nona and Granddad aren't pleased by much," Noah continued, watching the coffee drip. "Boss says I'm lucky they love me."

"Ah."

"We used to come here for a week in the summer, or for Passover, but I guess they were on really good behavior then because Boss made it clear that if they weren't, we wouldn't come back. I didn't notice until, like, last year."

"Parents and children..." Michaelis shrugged, a bit at a loss. It was very American, all this sharing, but then Noah was young and had grown up there.

"Sure, but I don't think Nona and Granddad even like *each other*. Wild, right?" Noah asked, turning around. "I wouldn't marry someone I didn't like."

"People get stuck, I suppose. My son considered an arranged marriage for a while. My fault, I pressured him. I forget not everyone marries young like I did."

"How old were you?" Noah asked.

"You should read more Shivadh history," Michaelis said with a smile. "I was nineteen."

"But you liked them, right?"

"Indeed, I loved her very much." Michaelis got up and picked up one of the mugs, pouring from the quarter-full pot, to avoid further discussion. "Well, I'm glad you're both here. And if you want to leave in autumn, a lot of places will open up. If you don't want to live in town, there are cabins in the highlands, too."

"Really just the one highland," Noah said, a fossilized old Shivadh joke, and Michaelis burst out laughing.

"Who taught you that old chestnut?" he asked.

"Eddie Rambler's Photogram."

"Bless. If you want to live in our one highland, I can make some recommendations."

"Who was laughing?" Jes asked, struggling through the front door with an enormous suitcase, the overalls they were wearing streaked with dust. Noah ran to help them. "I heard you from outside."

"Noah was entertaining me," Michaelis called. "Welcome to the lodge."

"Thank you, we'll try to keep being funny," Jes said, as Noah wrestled the bag away and carried it off. Michaelis poured another mug of coffee and passed it over. "Gorgeous. Noah and I will go out today and buy our own food. We wanted to leave early."

"Noah mentioned some strife," Michaelis said.

"Of course he did." Jes sighed. "Spilling our family drama…"

"Every family has some. Gregory used to enjoy dredging up old scandals from royal families past and sharing them over dinner, or doing reports on them for school. Nothing I haven't heard a dozen times before."

"I put your bag in your bedroom," Noah announced, returning. "And I checked the studio calendar, you have the whole afternoon off to unpack while Lachlan and I record with Michaelis."

"All business," Jes said fondly, ruffling his hair. "Let's at least have breakfast first. Actually, we were going to go out – can we buy you breakfast?" they asked Michaelis.

"I wouldn't mind. There's a little place down by the beach that does a traditional fried breakfast," Michaelis suggested. It was cheap and hot, and he felt like a bit of salt air this morning.

"An entire fried breakfast?" Noah asked.

"I still have the Jaguar here," Michaelis said.

"We'd have to strap Noah to the roof. No, come on, we'll take the van, and you can have a fried breakfast just this once," Jes said to Noah. Michaelis went to get his shoes, already pleased. He couldn't imagine why he hadn't thought of going down to the beach for a nice breakfast before now.

"Hello listeners! I'm Noah," Noah said, settled with ease in front of his mic.

"I'm Michaelis," Michaelis added.

"I'm Lachlan, hi!" Lachlan chimed in.

"And this is *How To Make Some Noise*," Noah finished. "Your weekly podcast about podcasts."

"So, Noah, tell everyone why I'm here," Michaelis said.

"Michaelis is the retired king of Askazer-Shivadlakia, and he's going to be making a show about his life and work," Noah said. "But how much do you know about podcasting?"

"Absolutely nothing," Michaelis confirmed.

"So my job is to get you up to speed on how a podcast gets made, and show everyone else how it's done as well. Next time we'll start at the very beginning, so everyone can follow along, but this time we're going to discuss our setup a little."

"Very first question: if you're the host and I'm your guest, what's Lachlan doing here, buried behind all that technology?" Michaelis asked.

"Aside from looking gorgeous?" Lachlan put in.

"Goes without saying," Michaelis intoned, and Lachlan laughed.

"In most recording studios, the producer who watches the audio levels and keeps us on track is in a separate room with a glass partition, so they can see us but won't make noise on the microphones," Noah said. "But we're recording in this awesome old bunker, which is mostly concrete, so we can't put any windows in and it's tough to run cords through the walls. Lachlan's going to stay cozy in here with us, and you'll all hear him occasionally."

"Not that I mind," Lachlan said. "More time to admire Michaelis."

"I'll try to remember to comb my hair," Michaelis replied.

They'd scripted this out, at least to an extent; Lachlan, rather sweetly in Michaelis's opinion, had asked if he felt all right about a little silliness over his looks, and he'd said he didn't mind, as long as it was clear it was all in fun. Nobody wanted to be condoning harassment on air, but a joke every now and then didn't hurt anyone.

"In a few episodes we'll come back to the technology in more detail," Noah said, launching into the meat of the show. "Lachlan is producing for us because he's been in radio for about ten years, the last three of those here in Askazer-Shivadlakia..."

It really was odd, Jes thought, how easy they found it to settle into a new routine. A few weeks into living at the lodge, it felt like they'd always been there; they knew where the laundry was and how to nudge the elderly fridge just right when the door wouldn't immediately open. Noah was slowly exploring every nook and cranny except for Michaelis's rooms, and he'd been out in the little boat moored at the lake dock a handful of times, alone but always under some kind of adult beachside supervision.

Often, in the mornings, Jes came into the kitchen to find Michaelis had already made coffee and gone out; aside from his old-fashioned morning athletics, they weren't sure what he did, but he didn't seem annoyed by their presence. Most evenings if they wanted to find him he was in the living room, reading.

Sometimes, when Noah got on a kick about experimenting with Shivadh cooking, he'd sit at the kitchen bar and watch, offering frequently useless suggestions until Noah made him text the palace chef for help. Jes had never met Simon, but probably owed him a couple of beers, the way Noah and Michaelis pestered him.

It was such a deep relief, too, not to wake up to their parents sniping at each other every morning – to pour some coffee, linger over the morning news before starting work on the various stories they were chasing, greet Michaelis when he came in from running or a morning swim, and make breakfast for Noah without criticism or commentary from anyone else. They felt…in control again, in a way they sometimes hadn't even in New York. There was something to be said for predictability, which twenty-year-old Jes would have laughed at, but twenty-year-old Jes didn't know who they were or what they wanted or how to get it. These days, they generally had a handle on at least two of the three.

As far as Jes knew, Noah's podcast with Michaelis was going well. They had their hands full with the rest of the network. They were long-distance supervising a few network podcasts still being made in New York, working on their own, and helping with the various clients coming into the bunker to do one-off recordings. A surprising number of locals were interested in recording audiobooks, either their own modest efforts or books for family who needed audio. There were even a few musicians, none especially promising but all very earnest. If Jes wanted to discover the next big star from Askazer-Shivadlakia, they supposed they'd have to wait until Eurovision like everyone else.

It was a busy life, but it was a living, and it had its little pleasures.

One of them was just coming in through the front door now – Michaelis, fresh from a swim in the lake, bare-chested with a towel over his shoulders, swim trunks still damp. Jes leaned on the counter and pretended to be engrossed in their coffee.

"Morning," Michaelis called, padding into the living room.

"Ah, morning," they replied, looking up. "Good swim?"

Hello, pectorals, Jes thought. *Greetings, biceps.*

"Middling. Looks like it's going to storm, so I got out early. I'm sure my obituary will be many things, but I hope it won't read *Former King Dies In Freak Lightning Strike*," he said.

"Good to know; I was thinking of going out today. If it's going to pour, I'll stay in."

"Storm should clear up soon. Good beach weather coming this week, I think. Have a good day in the studio," he added, passing down the hallway towards his suite.

Goodbye, ass. Adieu, calves.

Michaelis was exactly the kind of mistake twenty year old Jes would have made, an older man with a deep voice and a significant amount of power. New York was full of men like him and some of them were even as good-natured as he was, though not many. Jes suspected, however, that while his wife had passed he still thought of himself as married, not widowed, and married men were a mistake they had learned *not* to make.

In any case, he was literally making it possible for them to run their business, and that deserved caution too.

Still, Jes was old and wise enough to enjoy the view without needing to buy the property. If Michaelis didn't mind walking through the lodge in his swim trunks, Jes wasn't going to object.

Eddie emerged from the shower to the usual morning noise – Gregory moving around, dressing and drinking coffee, exchanging a few words with his valet before he got on with the day. Often he had the news on, but more frequently these days it was audio – back episodes of *The Echo*, or short daily podcasts about world events. This morning it was clearly a podcast, but it wasn't about the news, exactly.

"Is that Michaelis?" Eddie asked, over what sounded like

Gregory's father talking about microphones.

"It's the first episode of his show with Deimos's kid," Gregory replied. "It's great and also very weird to listen to."

"Is he flirting with that dude?" Eddie asked, eyes going wide as another male voice said something and Michaelis chuckled.

"Their tech guy, Lachlan," Gregory said. "That's what's a little weird."

"I didn't think your dad swung that way."

"As far as I'm aware, he doesn't, but he doesn't tell me everything. And remember, my love, we don't have the same hangups some Americans do. He wouldn't care if someone thought he was dating this fellow, it's no harm to him."

"But it's still weird for you?" Eddie asked.

"Hearing your father flirt with someone on a globally available medium wouldn't be weird for you?"

"Point. Are you okay with it? Because of your mom, I mean."

"I'm a little surprised he is, to be honest. I went to therapy, I've done the work," Gregory said. Eddie wrapped his arms around Gregory's waist, knocking his forehead gently against the back of Gregory's head. "When she died he just...kept working. I mean, it's possible he got some help and didn't say, but I don't think so. It's good to hear him having fun, anyway."

"Maybe he's getting some help now," Eddie said, gesturing at the speaker as Michaelis laughed.

"Maybe so," Gregory said, sounding pleased. "Either way, nice to hear. Haven't heard that in a while. Good for Dad."

CHAPTER FIVE

MICHAELIS AND NOAH seemed to be doing well with *How To Make Some Noise*, so Jes had tried to stay out of it. Noah was supposed to be helping Michaelis figure out his own podcast as well, but Jes didn't want to pressure either one of them. Michaelis didn't seem hurried, and Noah was a kid, not a pro they were paying to get the work done. If he did go into the family business, he'd need to know how to take initiative without a manager prodding him on. Prodding was Jes's job as a parent, not as a producer.

Still, whenever they knew Noah and Michaelis were talking about the show, they kept an ear cocked, and probably for the best. Sometimes you had to learn by failing, after all.

"I understand you're frustrated," they heard Michaelis say as they passed through the lodge one evening after dinner, and they stopped to listen to the two arguing in the kitchen. "I am trying, Noah."

"I know! That's what's so annoying. You are trying but we're not getting anywhere," Noah said.

"Then that's not my fault."

"I didn't say it was!"

"All right, well, what haven't we tried?" Michaelis said. "We've been brainstorming, clearly that hasn't worked. Maybe we should try coming at this from some other angle. How do I make things interesting without being indiscreet? How do I pick out what's interesting in the first place?"

"How can you not know what's interesting?" Noah demanded.

"It's my life, Noah, I lived through all of it, none of it seems all that compelling to me," Michaelis said, which was...actually rather worrying. It was the kind of thing Jes had heard depressed friends say, and they thought he'd moved past that a little.

"Hey," Jes said, leaning in the doorway. Both of them looked up, Noah visibly upset, Michaelis desperate. "This doesn't look like the book club I signed up for."

"Very funny, Boss," Noah muttered.

"Cranky," Jes said, going to him and rubbing the back of his head affectionately. He didn't bat them away, so he couldn't be too mad. "You're getting frustrated and Michaelis is getting tired."

"Well, he's being frustrating," Noah said.

"I'm sure he is, he probably had classes in how to frustrate people," Jes said, dropping Michaelis a wink. He nodded, tilting his head in understanding of what they were doing. "Which is all the more reason to tag out. You guys have been working on this for weeks. Why don't you let a pro handle this one."

"I could be a pro," Noah said rebelliously.

"Someday you will, but this calls for drastic measures only I can do safely," Jes said, rummaging in the fridge for a post-dinner snack. "Go be a kid for a while. You're off the clock."

Noah seemed to relax a little. Perhaps he needed the reminder more often. "Can I stay up and video chat with Mart?"

"Might as well," Jes agreed, pulling a handful of grapes off a bunch and eating them, one by one. Inspiration struck them and they smiled. "Go on, give Mart my love. Michaelis and I are going to play the questions game."

"Fine. But we're not done," Noah added to Michaelis.

"I never dreamed we were," he said, and Noah gave him a sharp nod and went off to the suite. "Who's Mart?" Michaelis asked when he was gone.

"One of my New York friends. She's a drag queen, and she's usually getting ready for work right around the time he goes to bed now, so to get to stay up and talk with her while she puts her makeup on is kind of a treat."

"Good. He deserves it after putting up with me. I forget how young he is."

"So does he," Jes sighed. "And then he loses his temper."

"He's trying to help," Michaelis said, circling to sit at the kitchen bar, on the other side from them. Perfect. "It's not his fault he's got very dry clay to work with."

"Nor his fault that he's fifteen," Jes said, finishing the grapes and washing their hands. "He's better at the technology than you but he hasn't got a lot of experience being a teacher."

"I'm out of practice as a student," Michaelis said.

"I don't really think you need to study," Jes replied. "What you need is something to knock yourself loose."

Michaelis spread his hands. "Your cunning plan?"

"The questions game." Jes went to a cupboard and took down a box they'd uncovered a few days before. "Found these. I assume they were for entertaining at some point. We are going to play a game I learned coming up in my journalism career."

Michaelis watched warily as they unpacked a set of shot glasses, lining them up in the middle of the counter. They each bore the royal crest. He picked one up and touched the crest thoughtfully.

"Now, you can just say no and walk away, and I will still respect you. But I think this will help, so I want you to keep an open mind," Jes said.

"A game, you say," Michaelis said, setting the glass down.

"It's a little like truth or dare. I'm going to try and help you figure out some really interesting stories to tell," Jes said. "Which can be uncomfortable."

Michaelis blinked again. "Hence the shots."

Jes produced, from under the counter, a gray-green bottle. Michaelis leaned back from it as if it had an evil aura.

"Shots of Davzda," Jes announced.

"Absolutely not," Michaelis replied.

"It's fine, it's the legal stuff."

"That doesn't make it better," Michaelis observed.

"It's a little better! The legal stuff hasn't got any psychedelics in it and it's only fifty percent alcohol by volume. Practically speaking, it's just gin," Jes told him.

"It tastes like beach sand," Michaelis said. "Goes down like it too."

"That's the salt content. It's medicinal," Jes continued, pouring out a series of shots. "You can't get this stuff in America, I had to import it while I lived there. Cheers," they added, and did a shot. It burned, tasting like bad decisions and yes, beach sand.

"You are going to die," Michaelis told them.

"Not me. So listen, here's how it works," Jes said, making soft little hacking noises around the words as the alcohol lingered. "I ask you uncomfortable questions. If you can, you answer them. If you don't want to answer, you have to do a shot."

Michaelis frowned. "What's this meant to accomplish?"

"You royals, so direct," they replied, getting water glasses down from the cupboard and filling them. "It's meant to ease you in, so that after a while you're drunk enough to answer the question anyway. And if you won't answer any questions, you pass out fast, don't waste my time, and get a hangover as punishment."

He seemed to study the shots in front of him. The fumes wafting off them were practically visible.

"I'd like to set some boundaries," he said finally.

"I wouldn't have guessed," Jes replied drily.

"Nothing about Gregory," he ticked the first rule off on his index finger, looking at them. They nodded.

"Fair, this isn't about him," they said.

"Nothing about my wife," Michaelis added, touching his middle finger with his thumb. "I'll talk about her if I please but she's not an open topic for an interview."

Jes felt their heart crack a little. "All right," they agreed.

"Thank you." He touched his ring finger with his thumb.

"And I'm allowed to pass without drinking if you ask anything that might threaten the security of the country."

"How would I know you're telling the truth?" they asked.

"I'm an honorable man," he answered. Jes gave him a skeptical look. "What? I did a great job here…" he gestured outward at the country. "I'm trusting you not to take advantage of me if I get alcohol poisoning from this…"

"I reserve the right to renegotiate," Jes said. "And if you can tell me off the record I want the tea."

"The tea," Michaelis snorted. "Fine. But on that note, nothing goes further than us without my permission, tomorrow, in the cold light of day."

"Smart," Jes said. "Agreed. You want a shot to start with?"

"I don't even want a shot to end with. I might get through this entirely sober," Michaelis declared.

"Who is the sexiest world leader you've met?" Jes asked.

Michaelis looked at them, looked at the shots, considered it, and downed one, no chaser. He didn't even wheeze, but his ears turned pink.

"All right, I'll softball you," Jes said, laughing. Michaelis folded his arms on the counter and gestured with one hand.

"Go on, then," he said.

The thing about the questions game was that it was really two games. There was the drinking game, of course – innocent but a little dangerous, maybe even a little sexy. Ultimately it felt fun, whether or not it was helpful in this case.

But the second game, Jes had learned, was a chess game, one the other person hopefully didn't know you were playing.

With Michaelis, the trick was to start out easy, with questions he could answer without feeling self-conscious – then throw in just a few that might make a shot seem attractive. Get him closer to doing at least one more shot, but never make it seem like too much at once. With Davzda involved and with him already on edge about the idea...

Michaelis looked askance at some of the early questions – *How did it feel to be crowned? What's the most boring story you have? Who do you think is the most famous person you've ever met?* – but every now and then Jes would throw in something which sounded innocent and which also made his eyes dart to the shot glasses.

He did his second shot half an hour in, his third ten minutes later, both regarding his opinion on certain world political figures. Jes pulled back then and gave him time to forget he already had the equivalent of about half a bottle of wine in him. They gave him a glass of water, made him drink most of it around more softball questions, and then said, "Okay, this is a little personal, but bear with me."

He gestured for them to continue.

"Why did you move out here to the lodge? And don't say it was for the fishing. You've got two fish in the freezer and haven't gone out on the lake since Noah and I arrived."

"Could have gone in the early morning and cooked them for breakfast," he pointed out. "You wouldn't even know."

"We'd smell the fish."

"Only if I caught any. Maybe they weren't biting," he replied. Then he shrugged and, without being prompted, continued. "Of course it's not for the fishing. If I can't tell a polite lie by now I shouldn't have ever been king."

Jes leaned forward, propping themself on the counter separating them from the former king. "So? Why?"

Michaelis studied the nearest full shot glass, then shook his head. "It was pragmatism. Gregory's very new on the throne, but he's more ready than I was – he's the first king in generations who actually got the right kind of training for the role. My father was naturally good at it and I was a quick study, but Gregory was both born and trained to do this kind of work."

"So?"

"So he ought to be given the chance to do it. People don't like change and they don't want to learn new ways of doing things. Can't have them come round looking for me when they should be talking to him. I go up and knock around in my old office sometimes in case anyone really needs me, and I stay up at the palace on weekends, but…" he shrugged. "Best if I fade into the wings for a while."

"Hm," Jes said, and he tilted his head.

"What, hm?" he asked.

"It makes me think of Jean Valjean," they said.

"How so?"

"Have you read *Les Miserables?*"

"No, the thing's a doorstop," Michaelis replied. "And I just don't care that much about France. But we had several touring versions of it come through, and I believe a few years ago a local school put on a production. That was…certainly an experience."

"So you know the basic plot, right?"

"More or less."

"At the end of the book, he's got his daughter settled in with her husband, and he's making sure she's taken care of," Jes said. "He figures his sordid past might someday come out, so he sets about making sure he can't taint her life with it. He won't even sign their marriage contract, he fakes a wound to get out of it. He moves away, starts making her call him by his name instead of father, that kind of thing. And he makes it…easier for her to lose him. Because he knows he's dying."

Michaelis seemed to consider this, distracted from earlier questions by the idea they'd suggested.

"I have no intentions of dying anytime soon," he said at last. "And I'd rather not distance myself from my only child that way. But there's this thing about being king, and I don't know if I can explain it."

Jes gestured at him to take his time. He nodded, chewing on

his lip.

"Gregory and I both joke about the Shivadh love of drama," he said. "A good kind of drama. The people want a show. You know," he said, and Jes nodded. They did know; the country probably only still had a king because it sounded more fun than having a president. "So, we are Shivadh. I'm not immune and he certainly isn't. There's a feeling you have as king, a connection to the country. Even an elected king, there's something different about it. You aren't only a politician. You think, this country is mine to care for, and if I'm lucky and good at it, it'll be that way for most of my life. I felt it, and I know Gregory does. I want him to get to experience that without me standing in the way, or even casting a shadow. And I'm a little jealous, because it's not mine anymore," he added ruefully.

"That's a staggering loss," Jes said. It was; it made their heart ache to think of it. It reminded them of leaving Askazer-Shivadlakia when they were young. To give it up when you were an angry child was one thing. To give it up after dedicating your life to it...

"Well, I don't love drama *that* much," Michaelis said dismissively, but he wouldn't look them in the eye.

"It is, though," Jes insisted. "You had a life's purpose, and you passed that on when you knew it was the right thing to do, but you still had to lose it. That's hard, and people shouldn't tell you it isn't."

"Nobody's told me that. Least of all Gregory," he said with a laugh. "I just – thought I'd come out here and lose myself for a little while, until that all subsided. All that...feeling."

"Has it?"

Michaelis looked at them, looked away, and then picked up one of the shots, grimacing as he downed it.

"Do you think it will?"

He shook his head and did another one, which was a lot even for a veteran of the game.

"Fair enough," Jes agreed. They picked up the bottle and two of the empty shot glasses. "Come on."

"Where are we going?"

"I'm tired of standing and those stools aren't very comfortable," Jes said, walking out of the kitchen. They could hear the stool's legs grate against the floor as Michaelis followed.

Jes settled on the floor, back against the sofa, and put the shot glasses on the coffee table, filling them both. Michaelis seemed to ponder this, then set down his water glass next to the shots and sank to the floor on the other side of the coffee table, gracefully, legs crossed. After brief consideration, he rested his arms on the table and leaned forward to put his chin on them. It was probably the most he'd slouched in years, Jes thought.

"I can see how you came to prominence as a journalist," he said. Jes gave him a gentle smile.

"I did that because I worked extremely hard and kissed a lot of ass," they said. "Go on then. Take a break, that was rough. Have some more water. Ask me a question."

"Hmf." He watched them with his dark eyes, considering while he took a sip of water. "Why did you leave Askazer-Shivadlakia, all those years ago?"

Jes thought about it, but they weren't quite ready to discuss that outside of a therapy office – and the point wasn't for them to share, not really, but to build trust.

They picked up a shot, gave him a look, and downed it.

"All right," he said. "When you came back, did you really move halfway across the world just to do a podcast?"

"If I wanted to cheat, I could just say no, and not elaborate," Jes pointed out. Michaelis was silent. "Also, that is such a politician question."

"I'm a politician."

"I'm well aware." They shifted a little, settling in. "No. For one thing, a podcast about Askazer-Shivadlakia is never going to be especially lucrative and I unfortunately do not have a large inheritance or a suspiciously dead rich spouse. I have some money, enough to do this, but not enough that I can stop working, or do just as I please."

"Then why?"

"A few reasons," Jes said. "The most significant was that Noah was struggling. He's such a smart kid, but he's awkward and too old for his years, which is probably my fault, and he just...couldn't find his place, in school, with his cohort. I thought, well, the schools here are better, they're smaller, and it's a chance for him to reinvent himself if he wants."

"He doesn't seem at all awkward to me," Michaelis said.

"Well, my friend, you are a grown man and kind of a nerd, of course you're a kindred soul," Jes pointed out. "I'm sure he'd get along well with your very nerdy son Gregory, too."

"Gregory Three," he murmured, and they didn't understand until he continued. "Gregory Two was his namesake. Nice man, so I'm told, but not a very good father. Raised an extremely useless son."

"Yes, I did have year three history," Jes chided gently.

"Sorry. Do go on."

"Go on with what?"

"You said Noah was the most important reason. As a father, I agree. As a king, I still want to know why else you came back. I don't get the impression it was patriotism."

Jes considered doing another shot, but hell, the odds of Michaelis even remembering this in the morning were slim.

"Your son is gay, and still took a very public job that complicated his life more than almost any other would," they said.

"Tell me about it," he replied.

"I respect that a lot. I know that this place is...more permissive – more accepting? I'm not even sure of the word," they admitted. "But it's kinder for someone like me, that was always true. Now there's this precious, fragile growing thing, this community here that people are trying to build, in a place that's good for us. To have a gay king is…a little patch of sunlight for people who need it to flourish. America is *so hard*, Michaelis, you have no idea. Everywhere can be hard but it felt like it was getting harder, in a way I didn't like and didn't want for my son. I didn't feel safe, either. Lachlan isn't even from here, but when he told me I needed to come back, he said I should come *home*. I thought, if Lachlan can feel like this is home, I might feel safe here too."

"Do you?"

"So far, yes," Jes said. "Doesn't hurt that I have a powerful patron."

"I don't like that word," he said. "Patron. I'm not patronizing you. I have no power."

"Of course you do. You've given us a place to work, a place to live. People in this country still look to your example."

"I'm not a powerful patron," he insisted.

Jes fought the urge to make a joke, because it did seem important to him. "Fine. You are…an influential friend. How's that?"

"Better," he agreed. He sat up straight, took one of the shots, and threw it back, without a question, without prompting. Jes refilled it calmly, hiding their surprise.

"Can I ask another?" they asked.

"Of course. That's the point, yes?" His smile was open and warm, unguarded, and it felt a little like a gift.

"Yes," they agreed. "What's the most important political lesson you learned, back when you were studying the other kings? What I mean is, what was most relevant to you, from them?"

"Difficult to say," he said thoughtfully. "I think…maybe the Echardt Scandal. Well, it's called that. I feel like it'd barely be considered sensational compared to what you see on Photogram, at least up to a point. In the memoirs you can read the story in the words of the royals who had to deal with it, and it taught me a lot about…a lot," he finished. "Echardt was a powerful man about three hundred years ago. He held some loans the king at the time had used to…I think he had financed a minor war."

"Oh, only a minor one," Jes said.

"We're a very small country, major ones happen without our input," Michaelis pointed out.

"I'm sorry, continue."

"Well, this Echardt kept a mistress, and also a…mister," Michaelis said. His speech was slower, less exact than usual, his vowels round and soft. "His man wrote to Echardt's wife, fed up with being second fiddle I suppose, and told her anonymously that her husband was being unfaithful. Doesn't seem very bright, if you ask me."

"Why not?"

"More likely to get the boyfriend dumped, eh? And if not that, get Echardt thrown out of his own home, and at that point he's less likely to keep a consort of any kind."

"I suppose that's true," Jes agreed.

"Anyway, wife goes to Echardt and says, is this true, he says no, of course not, and secretly dumps the boyfriend. Who, crucially, goes to the girlfriend."

"This definitely was not in the history books," Jes said.

"Bet it is if you know where to look," Michaelis replied, with a level gaze only slightly marred by the fact that he wasn't entirely focusing. "So the girlfriend goes to the wife in person and says her husband's playing an even wider field than she thought. Echardt doubles down. Absolutely not. Faithful to the end. Well. There's two women fighting with Echardt inside his house and one cheerleading ex-boyfriend standing outside, and the commotion got bad enough someone called whatever passed for law enforcement back then. Whole thing came in front of the king. Out of deference to Echardt, it was in private, more or less."

"To the debts Echardt held, I think you mean."

"Which is also why the king said that the man should sort out his business himself. He knew he didn't want to cross the man holding his loans. He knew that the consorts didn't have the means to cause a real fuss and the wife could be, ah, stifled."

"Gross."

"Undoubtedly. But the wife turns out to know secrets both royal and financial, and it gets fiddly here," Michaelis continued, fingertips dancing around the table. "I'd have to look up what exactly went on. The girlfriend and boyfriend both left town, which was a smart decision. The wife eventually put the screws to Echardt and said, either you sign it all over to me and leave too, or I'll bring you down by force with what I know."

"Do we...do we know her name?" Jes asked. "I have a statue I'd like to put up."

He put a finger to his lips. "Sh. Let me tell it. Echardt tells his wife he's not leaving and if she tries to end him he'll kill her. She pitches a fit – I would too – and it comes back to the king. King's obviously not pleased at all by this."

"Why? Seems like either way, he gets rid of this asshole."

"You'd think," Michaelis said. "But remember, this is all happening more or less in private, which starts to look more and more like a cover-up. People know the king is close with Echardt but not why. King says to Echardt, I told you to fix this yourself. Echardt thinks this time if he hints about the loans the king will support him and, like a fool, the king panics and does. He tells the wife, if she publishes she can be sure she *will* be damned."

"What did she do?"

"She published," Michaelis said with relish. "Made all his papers public and wisely went into hiding. Echardt fled with the clothes on his back. But that's not why it was so important. One of the papers indicated that not only did Echardt hold debts wildly beyond what was publicly known, but some of the loans the king took out didn't make it to the military."

"Where did they go?"

"The boyfriend."

Jes let out a little gasp. "The boyfriend was double-timing him with the king?"

"The boyfriend was blackmailing the king."

"Fuck!"

"I know!" he said. "So here's the kingdom now broke, the king's been caught paying off some banker's boyfriend for lord knows what reason, the banker's fled, the boyfriend's fled. The people are furious. And of course, the wife is essentially ruined. She got her revenge, but the money's obviously not coming back now. She can't stay in hiding from the king forever and she has limited time in which to harness the anger of the citizenry. So she does what any resourceful woman would do."

"Oh do tell," Jes said.

"Off with his head."

"What?" Jes asked, shocked.

"She raises an army, deposes the king, has him beheaded, and takes the throne."

Jes blinked at him, trying to formulate a response. After a while, they said, "So there might already be a statue of her."

Michaelis dissolved into laughter.

"No statue," he said, snorting with glee. "Maybe there should be. There are a couple of very good portraits in the palace. Her name was Queen Alekha. Dozen-or-so times great-grandmother of my wife, Miranda, actually."

"Well, don't mess with your wife's family," Jes said.

"One of the many lessons this has to teach us," Michaelis said. "But there were others. Everything I did as king, in those early years, I thought about the king who wanted to make Echardt sort this out himself. If I thought something was best handled in secret, I did it in public. If I thought it would be a bother to fix a problem that touched on the safety of the country, I made certain I never let it out of my sight. A king isn't there to make pronouncements, he's there to run the damn country."

"His personal dignity and safety be damned?" Jes asked.

"He is no longer a person. He's a king. At least, from eight to six every day. Outside of that, his duty is to those he loves.

Echardt and the king together did everything wrong. I'm not in support of beheadings, obviously, but…"

"Fuck around and find out," Jes said.

"A very succinct lesson I took very much to heart," he finished. "If you like that story, remind me to tell you sometime about my theory that Meyer Lansky saved the country from the Nazis during the war. Or the reason the town is called Fons-Askaz. Noah would call that one *wild*."

Jes stared at him. There was something here, something percolating, and when it bubbled to the surface they grinned.

"What?" Michaelis asked.

"This is it," they said. "This is the podcast."

He looked around. "Isn't," he replied. "You don't even have Noah's little pocket recorder."

"No, I mean conceptually. That's how you make this podcast. Okay, so maybe some of the stories you want to tell you can't, and some of the stories you ought to tell are interminably boring. But you still do have stories to tell. You tell a short version of a story from your life, maybe redacted if you have to, and then you talk about how history got you there. Or you start with a historical story and link it to one of yours. People eat that up," they finished. "You've named at least three of those stories you could tell just in the last fifteen minutes."

Michaelis took a while to mull this over, or possibly he'd lost his train of thought. Finally he looked up at them, glassy-eyed.

"So this is good," he said.

Jes grinned at him. "Oh, you are tanked."

Michaelis nodded gravely, very slowly, swaying a little where he sat. Jes laughed.

"Well, a breakthrough means success, we can finish for the night," they said, downing the last shot on the table. Michaelis tried to stand and made it most of the way up before he staggered. Jes caught his arm and steadied him; he leaned in against them, warm and close. His head bent forward, face tilting over theirs.

"Hi, Jes," he said softly.

"Hey, stranger," they replied, trying to stay light, trying not to think about how easy it would be to kiss him. It would also be taking advantage – and unwise even sober. "Come on. I'll walk you home."

"That's funny, because it's twenty feet in that direction," he informed them.

"Yes, I was aware," Jes agreed, gently moving him forward. They got a shoulder under his arm, wrapping their arm around his waist in order to guide him down the hall to the suite. He leaned against the wall outside the bathroom while they rummaged for painkillers, handing two pills to him with another glass of water and watching as he downed them.

"All of it," they said, and he obediently finished the glass. He stumbled into the bedroom and settled on the edge of the bed, unbuttoning his shirt.

"Can you get undressed all right?" they asked. Michaelis nodded, then nearly fell off the bed. "Well, if you fall over, try to land on a rug."

He gave them a warm grin, then a wave of a hand to show he'd heard and understood the joke. Jes turned to go, but just as they reached the door, he called, "Jes?"

"Mm-hm?" they asked, turning around again.

"This was…a good idea," he said, apparently measuring his words. "A terrible, good idea."

"I'm full of those," they agreed.

"I'm glad you're here, you and Noah," he said. "It's usually very empty. Very quiet."

"I'm glad too," Jes said. "Goodnight, Your Grace."

"Night," he agreed.

CHAPTER SIX

THE NEXT MORNING Jes woke late, but not too hung over. They staggered out into the kitchen to make coffee, not expecting Michaelis to have done it, but Noah was up first and had put it on to brew. They sat down across from him at the little dining table, nodding thanks over the lip of the cup.

"How'd it go?" Noah asked, shoveling cereal into his mouth. "Sorry about yesterday."

"Don't worry about it. Tempers get a little high sometimes. Michaelis is a dad, he understands. He won't hold it against you."

"Well, I'll tell him sorry too later."

"That would be a good thing to do," Jes said encouragingly. "Anyway, he ought to be in good spirits if he's not absolutely miserable with a hangover. We made progress."

"That fast? Way to make me feel great, Boss."

"It's my job to instill crippling self-esteem issues in you, isn't it?" Jes asked innocently.

"It's an unfair advantage that when you interview someone you get to use alcohol."

"Boy is it ever, just wait until you're older," Jes said. "Do you want the elevator pitch for his podcast or not?"

"Sure. Maybe even the five-minute taxi-ride pitch."

Jes smiled and pitched the concept to him the way they would a producer, something Noah hopefully would be one day if he went into broadcasting. He listened attentively, nodding, and took time to consider it when Jes was done.

"I like it, but I think you should do the show with him instead of me," he said finally, finishing his breakfast. "We can keep on doing *Noise* together, but you should do the history one with him. I can't keep up with that much research when I'm in school."

"You think he's up for something this research-intensive himself?"

"I mean, what else is he doing?" Noah gestured around the lodge with his spoon.

"Good point. Would you like to produce for it?"

"I can do it until school starts. Maybe Uncle Lachlan can after that. We should have *Noise* wrapped by then and I can focus on *Echo Junior*. I wonder if Michaelis would introduce me to Eddie Rambler if I asked," Noah said. "You know if he shouted out the podcast it could really spike our numbers."

"Nothing hurt by asking, though I wouldn't get my hopes up. I'm sure Rambler's a busy man," Jes replied. "What are you up to today?"

"Editing for *Echo Junior*. Can you come with me into town later?"

"Sure, I need to get groceries. Run along, entertain yourself."

"I usually do." Noah put his bowl in the sink, gave them a quick hug around the shoulders, and ran off to fulfill his destiny, or whatever it was he did when they weren't paying attention. Jes focused on coffee, eventually on breakfast and the morning news, and by the time they looked up again it was ten in the morning.

Even hung over, Michaelis should probably be up and moving around by now, but Jes hadn't heard anything. They supposed they should bring him some coffee, as compensation for the shots the night before; after considering for a moment they poured out a mug, added a dash of cream to approximate how he liked it, and went down the hall, rapping gently on his suite door.

"Come in!" his deep voice came through the door, and Jes pushed it open.

They expected to see him still in bed, or suffering in the chair by the window. Instead he was sitting on the neatly made bed, legs crossed. He was in a pair of dove-gray pajamas, the same shade as his hair, and he had a book open in his lap, reading spectacles perched on his nose. He looked like a professor having a leisurely Sunday morning.

"Brought you some coffee," they said, holding the mug up. "It's past ten, I thought you might be too hungover to move."

He looked up, eyes wide. "Past ten already?"

Jes nodded at the clock on the wall. Michaelis blinked but accepted the coffee.

"I woke up still drunk," he said, closing the book and setting it aside. "Don't think I've done that since my twenties."

"College?" they guessed.

"Mm, no, first Purim as king."

"Oh lord."

"Thank goodness there's no video. Anyway, I wanted to look up the details of that story I told you, about Queen Alekha? Got distracted by her biography."

"Great story," they said, leaning against the bedside table.

"Yes, but I don't like not remembering the details. So damn much to remember once you get to my age," he said. "I raided the books we have here but I'll need to go up to the library to get the proper citations. Mostly sober by now, I could go soon."

"I'm surprised you remembered telling me the story."

"Well, I don't remember getting to bed, so I probably owe you a thank-you," he said.

"You already did."

"Excellent. Thank you for making me drink water, too. The headache is mild, though it may be stubborn," he added, rubbing his forehead. "Only what I deserve, I imagine."

"Are there many stories like that one about Queen Alekha? That you know of, I mean."

"Oh, more than a few. Probably many I don't know of, as well. I mentioned Meyer Lansky, didn't I? I'll see what I can bring back from the library today on a few of them. You and Noah working?"

"I'm taking Noah into Fons-Askaz this afternoon, but nothing much otherwise. Want some company in the library?"

"Very much, if you'd like. It's a nice walk up to the palace, and Simon will be pleased to be able to make us some lunch."

"I would like that, I think," Jes replied, smiling. Michaelis smiled back. "Feels good, eh?"

"What's that?"

"Having a hook. When you figure out exactly how to get the story told."

"Yes, I suppose it does. How does one do it from here? Like a book report?"

"Try it like Noah said. Write a speech," Jes suggested. "From there we'll work out how to turn it into a dialogue."

He nodded, sliding off the bed. "I'll be going up in about half an hour. Meet you on the porch?"

Jes left him to dress, packing a bag for the walk to the palace. Pocket recorder, just in case; notebook, phone, and charger. They did a quick check of their hair to make sure it was fine, then after a brief consideration in the mirror they added a little highlighter to their cheeks, darkened their eyebrows, and considered lip gloss before deciding against it.

The day was warm and Michaelis seemed inclined to be quiet on the walk along the lake, so they left him to his thoughts. The palace came into view slowly, through the trees and up a slight incline. When they passed into it through a side entrance, the halls were cool and quiet.

"Parliament's in session, but it's across the building, we shouldn't be disturbed," Michaelis said, leading them through the corridors. "I think – "

"Father!" someone called, and the king of Askazer-Shivadlakia emerged from the other direction, looking startled. Michaelis stopped, as startled as the king, and then...

Jes watched Michaelis light up, subtly but unmistakably, at the sight of his son. His shoulders squared a little, his smile went wide, and his eyes grew more animated.

"Gregory! I thought you'd be in session," he said, clapping Gregory III on the shoulders.

"We're on a short recess. I didn't know you were here today! We should get lunch, later, if you'll be around. Eddie and Simon are experimenting with molasses, which should be exciting," the king said. His eyes darted curiously to Jes.

"Ah, I'm doing some research," Michaelis said. "This is Jes Deimos, I mentioned – "

"The podcaster!" Gregory beamed at them. "Yes, I've been listening. You're doing the show on Askazer-Shivadlakia and helping Dad with the memoirs project."

He bowed in the Shivadh fashion, deep to demonstrate respect, and Jes debated curtsying, then bowed back. To their shock, as they came out of the bow, the king winked.

"Always glad to see an expat coming home," he said. "We need people like you here. Your interview with Esta was food for thought. And I am working...slowly," he added with a grimace, "on the housing issue. Are you here for long? At the palace, I mean. You should come to lunch too."

Michaelis raised his eyebrows, a question on his face; the message was clear enough, that they didn't have to actually *dine with the king* if Jes didn't want to.

On the other hand, Jes hadn't got where they were in life by saying no to things like that.

"I'd love to," Jes said.

"Great. I'm going to go harass people who need harassing. One o'clock? Yes? Be prepared for barbecue sauce," the king said, and ran up the stairs two at a time. Jes watched him go, a little bemused, then turned back to Michaelis.

"I may not have mentioned he's a fan," Michaelis said. "Or, at least, an avid listener."

"Is it going to be strange if I'm there for lunch?" Jes asked.

"I don't see why it would be. Last time I had lunch with him,

Edward and my nephew Gerald made him mediate an argument about Hot Pockets."

"Has he ever eaten a Hot Pocket?"

"I'm not entirely clear on what they are, to be honest," Michaelis admitted.

"You didn't arrange this, did you?" Jes asked, as they began to climb the stairs.

"What, an introduction? No. I meddle in his life now and again when it matters, but I try to keep out of it unless he's truly flailing. And I assumed if you needed my help getting someone in the palace to listen to you, you'd ask."

"Thank you. Safe assumption to make."

"Through here," Michaelis said, pushing open the door of the palace library. "Let's see if we can find some primary sources on Queen Alekha."

When Eddie Rambler walked into the royal dining room for lunch that day, he was met with a full table: Gregory, one of his MPs, the King Emeritus, Alanna, and a stranger Eddie didn't recognize, but someone he definitely wanted to meet. He pushed the wheeled cart in front of him into the room and began unloading bowls of barbecue sauce onto the table, followed by a platter of roasted chicken and a sheaf of paper.

"I have six kinds of barbecue sauce and I'm going to need you all to fill out a survey," he announced. "Simon and I are having a difference of opinion regarding traditional Shivadh sauce, and half the internet is going to start setting cars on fire if we don't resolve it soon. It's Esta, isn't it?" he asked the MP.

"Good to see you again, Eddie," Esta said.

"You I have not met, but your hair is spectacular," Eddie added to the stranger, who had ice-white hair piled on top of their head in a fabulous pompadour.

"Dad brought a guest for lunch," Gregory said, accepting a kiss on the cheek and a hefty plate of chicken. "This is Jes Deimos, they're staying at the fishing lodge."

"Oh! And doing the shows we've been listening to. Nice to meet you. I also like your voice," Eddie said cheerfully, setting out the sauces. "Do you eat chicken? I can grab some crudites if not."

"Chicken is fine," Jes said, smiling at him. "Nice to meet you. My son and I both follow your Photogram."

"Cool! Here, help yourselves," Eddie said, putting spoons in the sauces. "Left to right, sweet to savory. I'm not saying where Simon or I fall on the issue, so that you can be impartial."

He settled in as they began passing the food around, sampling carefully and thoughtfully. Alanna was on her tablet, not unusual, but Gregory seemed in good spirits and Esta was pretty fun when she wasn't talking politics. Michaelis was quiet, but he often was. Eddie had recently observed to Gregory that his father was the definition of still waters running deep, and Gregory had laughed and agreed.

"You're recording out at the fishing lodge now, aren't you?" Eddie asked Jes, leaning in to be heard over the conversation going on around them.

"His Grace really scored points with my son on that one," they said, nodding. "He's over the moon to be recording in a historical bunker, and he loves the lake. Of course, it's been helpful from a practical standpoint, too."

"I heard about the storm, but only what you put on the podcast and second-hand information from Greg. I'd have paid a lot to see His Grace running through the rain with a soundboard," Eddie said with a grin. Jes laughed.

"It was more than I expected to see," they agreed. "Worked out well for us in the end. The lodge is beautiful."

"I've done some filming at the lake. Gorgeous country."

"You really do like it here, don't you?" Jes asked. "That's not an act for those tourism bits you do."

Eddie nodded. "Simon – the royal chef, kind of a partner in crime – he told me that after he arrived, he couldn't ever leave. I know the feeling. We're still figuring everything out but I'm liable to be here a while. From the sound of it, you have more complicated feelings about the country, though."

"It's different when you're born here, I suppose," Jes said. "Born here and not a royal, anyway," they added.

"I can imagine. We're keeping exalted company now, though, huh?"

"Or they're slumming it, I haven't decided."

Eddie grinned, delighted. "Oh, I'm going to drop that idea on Gregory at some point. He'll be enraged. Love to enrage him," he added fondly. "Making one of the royal family lose their temper, even if it's just in fun, feels like a real accomplishment."

"Tell you a secret?" Jes asked, and Eddie nodded eagerly. "I got Michaelis to play a drinking game last night."

"Wait, really?"

"He did shots! It was *great*. Do recommend. He's funny when you loosen him up a little."

Michaelis had terrorized Eddie the first time they'd met, but with time and experience he'd come to realize it probably hadn't been intentional. And anyway, Gregory and Alanna were both worried about him lately.

"Probably did him a world of good," Eddie said. "He's been struggling a little, Gregory thinks."

"I got that sense, yes. But we're making great headway on his podcast now."

"Well, if you need a hand from the palace…Michaelis has a lot more pull than I do, but I'm here," Eddie said. "Always happy to help."

"Actually, it's not exactly what you're offering, but I was wondering if you'd consider coming on one of the podcasts," Jes said. "Noah'd give an arm to have you on *Echo Junior*."

Eddie nodded. "Sure, that'd be a kick. Who should I talk to

about scheduling?"

"I'll have Noah get in touch. What's a good way to reach you?"

They were in the middle of exchanging information when Eddie caught Michaelis watching them; he had an expression on his face that was difficult to read, but it was a reminder that this was a man who'd known Eddie was dating Gregory for weeks before saying anything. He had an awareness of the people around him that bordered on uncanny, and a career politician's sense of when to deploy it.

"So, Your Grace," he said, when Michaelis saw him looking. "Are you Jes's boss, or are they yours, now?"

"I think I'm either client, student, or building superintendent, depending on time of day," Michaelis replied.

"Don't forget barista," Jes added. "He rises at dawn, which is extremely unsettling, but it does mean there's usually coffee in the kitchen when I drag myself awake. I was alarmed when he wasn't around this morning but it turns out he just got lost in research."

"Which reminds me, I'd like another hour or so in the library this afternoon," Michaelis said, pushing back from the table. "Jes, if you'd like to head back to the lodge, I'd understand."

"No, I'll come with you," they said. "But then I do have to get home. Noah wanted me to go into Fons-Askaz with him this afternoon."

"Right. If you'll excuse us – Your Majesty," Michaelis added to Gregory with a bow. Jes said their goodbyes and followed him out, and Eddie sat back in his chair, relaxing slightly.

"Well, you made a friend," Esta said. "Gregory asked me along because I know Jes, and he was worried they'd feel a little at odds, but you kept them occupied. Not that I mind either way. Not every day you get to have barbecue chicken with two kings."

"I like Jes. I've been very charmingly roped into appearing on their kid's podcast," Eddie said. "And then your dad just glared the shit out of me, Greg."

"You'd think you'd be used to it by now," Alanna said.

"He hasn't glared at me in weeks, at least!"

"No, he hasn't," Gregory said, eyes slightly narrowed, still on the doorway.

"Greg," Eddie said, half a question.

"Mm?" Gregory looked at him, then shook his head. "Sorry. Just strange to see Dad cheerful again."

"Gregory," Alanna said, sounding a little appalled.

"You're the one who thought he was depressed! Eddie, I want you to spy for me," Gregory said. "When you're down at the lodge to do the podcast, just...see how he's doing."

"On it," Eddie agreed. "I love it when he gives me jobs," he told Esta.

"It's lost its novelty when he does it to me," she replied.

"All right, subjects," Gregory said. "Off with you all. Leave your questionnaires with Eddie. Eddie, go entertain yourself," he added, leaning over to kiss him. "Tell Simon whatever he thinks is right, I support him."

"Traitor," Eddie replied affectionately.

"Can't be a traitor when you're the king!" Gregory called as he walked out the door.

Michaelis had really only intended to make a few last notes and clean up, but as soon as he and Jes were back at the little study desk, Jes settled in with one of their finds and took their notebook out. He shrugged to himself and sorted the books into stacks – one pile to be left behind with a note not to be moved, one pile to take back with him, and one pile that could safely be given to the librarian to be re-shelved. The early afternoon light streamed in through the windows, warming his back. It dappled Jes, sitting in the chair across from his, turning their white hair subtly gold.

He'd enjoyed lunch, but seeing Eddie charm Jes so effortlessly, the way he seemed to do everyone – even Michaelis, who was fond of him and certainly felt Gregory could do worse – well, it had raised some kind of tension in him that he wasn't comfortable with. It wasn't anger or annoyance, and not jealousy precisely. Perhaps envy. Not of either one of them, though, which was what was perplexing him. It was the sense that he'd found…something interesting, something unique, and now the rest of the world also knew about it, when he'd thought he was the only one.

Ludicrous, of course. Jes wasn't some bauble that had washed up on the beach. In any case, plenty of people knew how interesting they were. They made their living being interesting for people. He supposed it wasn't that different from his own career.

He'd done a little research on them after they'd started working in the bunker, even before they and Noah had moved into the lodge. It only made sense to vet people who were in such close proximity, and if he hadn't done it, sooner or later someone at the palace would have. Probably had, in fact – he'd be willing to bet Gregory had a dossier on them on his desk, whether he'd looked at it or not.

Not that it would contain much to be concerned about. Jes Deimos was Shivadh-born with a US resident visa; they'd left Askazer-Shivadlakia at sixteen (that was a little surprising, but made sense in retrospect) and worked mostly odd, under-the-table jobs until their mid-twenties, when they'd gone to college. After that it was a somewhat distinguished career, first as a journalist and writer, then in audio media. They'd written a book of essays that had middling reviews, and sold a film script of some kind at some point, though it didn't appear to have been produced. They had a following in America that was significant enough they could live on revenue from advertising on the podcast network. He gathered few were so fortunate.

Noah had been born in the US, but children born outside

Askazer-Shivadlakia to at least one Shivadh parent were still citizens themselves, so he had all his paperwork in order – national healthcare card, youth ID, even a youth worker's permit so he could draw pay with the podcast network. He'd be enrolling in school in Askazer-Shivadlakia when the term began in October. Jes was the only parent listed on his Shivadh birth certificate. Whoever his other parent was, they didn't appear to be in the picture.

So, that was the family Deimos – comfortable but not wealthy, working hard for what they got. Famous in a very niche and specific way, not unlike himself. Jes was referred to in interviews and by interviewees as a kind person with an intellect like an ice pick, and now Michaelis saw why. He didn't remember all of the previous night but he remembered enough to know that he'd been drinking with someone who was fifteen years younger than him and absolutely on his level when it came to dissecting what it was people felt, thought, and wanted. The politician said it wouldn't do to get on their bad side. The man was intrigued.

Jes was bent over the book, slim shoulders tilted a little where their head was turned to study the page. They looked like someone Degas might have painted, if he'd been around for the 21st century. Perhaps Caillebotte.

He cleared his throat softly, and they looked up.

"If you want to take Noah into town before the shops start threatening to close for the day, we should go," he said. "You can take a few books with you if you like – I plan to."

"Oh, thanks," they said, closing the book and stretching. Michaelis flicked his eyes away. "I think for now mine can stay here. You know at lunch I got Eddie Rambler to consider doing a spot on *Echo Junior*?" they added, as he led the way towards the door. "Don't tell Noah, I want to spring it on him at dinner."

"Good for your podcast, I think," Michaelis said, descending the stairs.

"Great for it, if he's willing to promo it. And he seems like a nice guy."

"I think so. He adores Gregory, so in my opinion he has excellent taste."

Jes laughed. "Picking out china patterns?"

"The palace has plenty of china," Michaelis replied, which made Jes laugh harder. They stepped out into the humid summer air and, to his surprise, Jes put out their hand, palm up.

"What?" he asked, staring at it.

"Give me your books," they said.

"Why on earth?"

"Because I want you to discuss what you learned about the Echardt scandal, and you talk with your hands," they replied.

"I do?" Michaelis said, frowning, but he put the books in their hands.

"When you get excited, mostly. Has nobody ever mentioned it?" Jes asked. "And if you've got something in your hands while you're talking, you get annoyed by it."

"My father did that, too, come to think of it — moved his hands a lot, I mean. Now I'm trying to think if Gregory does it."

"No. Well, not exactly. I don't know him very well, obviously, but he *likes* to have things in his hands when he talks. Waves his fork around and stuff," Jes said. "You're very kinetic, both of you."

"Are you sure?" Michaelis asked, and then noticed with mounting perplexity that even as he asked it, he turned his right hand over, palm up, a questioning gesture. Jes's eyes went from his hand to his face, then back to his hand. "Well. That's unsettling to learn at an advanced age."

"Pfft. You're what, fifty?"

"Sixty-one."

"Get out of town."

"I'm afraid so. But thank you," he said, pleased by their disbelief.

"I've been doing some very incorrect math. Well, you look

fifty and might be sixty-one but you keep talking like you're ninety. In America, you'd technically be taking an early retirement, slacker," Jes teased.

"Fair enough," he said, falling back on self-deprecation. "I've been useless since leaving office."

"I don't know what's so bad about being useless, anyway, doesn't seem like such a sin to me," Jes said. Michaelis felt himself stop, shocked by the idea. Jes stopped too, turning to look at him. "What?"

"I...nobody's said that before," he said, confusion washing over him. "Usually it's some kind of platitude. Or a reassurance I'm still necessary. Nobody's just...said I could be useless and that was fine."

"For what it's worth, you're actually being extremely useful to me, but you don't have to be. I love being useless. A week's vacation doing nothing on the sofa? Favorite thing in the world," they said.

"And here I am making more work for you," he pointed out.

"Don't worry, I'll still find time to be a drain on society at some point," they replied, turning and continuing down the path. "Come on, keep up. Noah's going to start texting me soon if I don't get back."

He hurried to catch up, but he couldn't think of a single word to say.

"Echardt," Jes prompted gently.

"Right! Right," Michaelis said, and started talking, putting his thoughts in order as he went. It still wasn't a coherent telling, but he could feel the story taking shape, little turns of phrase here and there that he'd have to remember later. The research had been good, and repeating the story was helping. Jes mostly listened, his books tucked under their arm, a faint smile on their face. It *was* nice not to have books in his hands while he talked.

Noah was out on the dock in front of the lodge when they returned, feet in the water, playing some game on his phone, apparently without a care in the world. Michaelis looked at the boy and wondered if he'd ever been so young. If he had, it was hard to remember.

"Come on, kid, put some shoes on and get the keys," Jes called, and Noah hopped to his feet. "His Grace has homework and I promised you a trip into town. Unless you want to come," they added, turning to Michaelis.

"No – as you say…" he gestured at the books they were still carrying, and they put them back in his hands. "Have fun."

"Bye, Michaelis!" Noah called, running for the van, pulling his shoes on as he went. "See you for dinner maybe!"

Michaelis waved them off and headed inside, reflecting on how much the Deimos family filled the place, and how quiet they left it when they were absent.

They'd been in the van for all of thirty seconds when Noah said, "You know, I thought carrying someone's books when you like them was, like, something people in the forties did."

"He talks with his hands," Jes replied. Well, it'd worked on Michaelis.

Realistically, they'd missed out on that kind of thing when they were in school – carrying someone's books when you liked them, even if you'd rather die than act on it. Partly because of who they'd been, partly because they'd left school a little too early, grown up a little too fast. It felt good to finally get to do it. A little thrilling that Michaelis had allowed it.

"Sure, don't they all," Noah replied. "Uncle Lachlan's going to lose his mind."

"Uncle Lachlan's not going to hear about it from you, is he?" Jes asked.

"What, like he's going to judge you? He thinks Michaelis is good looking and fun. They're always bantering on the podcast."

"Michaelis *is* good looking and fun, yes, and it was very nice to carry his books. But you know you don't always have to act on that kind of thing."

"Again, this talk?" Noah asked.

"I want you to internalize that just because someone is good looking doesn't mean they're good for you."

"I'm pretty sure you've said on the podcast, on record, that they can still be a good time, though," Noah pointed out.

"That was a mature podcast and I am shocked, shocked and dismayed, that you have listened to a podcast rated 17+," Jes said.

"I edited that episode."

"Which is why I didn't get more explicit. Listen, Noah, I know that brain of yours is still growing, but do a little mental weight-lifting and tell me how you think flirting with the former king of the country you just moved to would go."

"How about I do a little mental weight-lifting and point out you already are?" Noah asked. "I'm not mad about it. I like Michaelis. He got us the studio and a place to stay."

"And do you want me to endanger that?" Jes asked.

"Oh," Noah said.

"Oh," Jes agreed. "Look. We both like him. It's a little weird for me because I also think of him as the king of my country, but I can see the human under the crown. I think his podcast is going to be pretty cool and I like being his friend. Maybe flirting a little. But a friend is all I'm going to be, for both our sakes."

"What if he likes you back?"

"I think Michaelis still misses his wife," they said. "I don't think he's looking for more from anyone else. And if he is, well, I'll figure that out if he acts on it. No use making plans for something that probably won't happen."

"You're not going to discourage him by carrying his books," Noah said loftily, and Jes shook their head and smiled.

CHAPTER SEVEN

"ARE WE HOT?" Jes asked, pointing at the mic, and Lachlan replied, "Just the hottest."

"Fantastic," Jes said, while Michaelis grinned at Lachlan.

"Ready to go, then?" Michaelis asked.

"Almost. But first, I have a present for you," Jes said, taking a paper bag from under the table.

"What on earth for?" Michaelis asked. "Is this a podcast tradition? I didn't think to get anyone gifts."

"Not exactly. And normally I would never recommend what we're about to do, so don't tell Noah that I'm setting a bad example," Jes told him. "But you know, the only real reason this podcast exists is that you and I were drinking together. And it was over drinks that we figured out how to make it work."

"Yes…" Michaelis said warily.

"So. This is our new tradition to open the show," Jes said, and thunked down two shot glasses from the bag.

"Oh, oh no, Jes – "

"Oh yes!" Jes said, producing a tiny gray-green bottle of liquor. "I promise I'll pour lightly."

"We are not doing *shots* before we even start," Michaelis said, as Jes poured two very shallow shots. "This is Davzda, this is a terrible idea."

"Well, then here's to terrible ideas," Jes said, lifting their shot. Michaelis groaned and picked his up, tapping it against theirs.

"Dozine," he said, a traditional Davzda toast, and drank when they did. "It tastes more dreadful every time."

"Clears the throat for talking, though," Jes said, and coughed as if to prove it. "Three, two, one. I'm Jes Deimos, creator and host of *The Echo* and executive producer of Reverb Podcast Network."

"I'm Michaelis ben Jason, King Emeritus of Askazer-Shivadlakia and recent poisoning victim," Michaelis said.

"This is your guide to Shivadh royal history, and we call it...*All On Mike*," Jes said, their voice deep with amusement.

"Still can't abide that name," Michaelis muttered, but loud enough for the mic to catch it. Jes just laughed.

Lachlan said, "Give me a brief hold for theme music..." and then when he pointed at them, Jes launched into the start of the script.

The first episode of *All On Mike* ("Don't Mess With Alekha") went up a few weeks later on a Thursday, because Thursday was the day for that kind of thing, apparently. Michaelis very carefully did not ask about numbers. Still, Noah spent all day wandering in and out of the lodge, announcing mysterious things like "Engagement is sky high" and "Someone said you sound like Benedict Cumberbatch's cool dad."

They'd left the "cold open" in, where Jes convinced him to do the shot of Davzda, and late in the afternoon Noah came in and said, "Davzda is trending. I bet the king's going to be furious."

"Why would Gregory be furious?" Michaelis asked.

"Everyone's trying to get some after hearing you talk about it. They're sold out in town. There were like, five bottles in all of America and one of them just sold online for six hundred dollars. Bet you tomorrow all the trendy food websites will have Davzda cocktail recipes."

"Well, a lot of people will die, but these are the sacrifices we make," Michaelis said.

"So there's going to be a shortage because all the sellers will export," Noah said. "Demand way up, but supply stays the same. Or if they hike supply, they can't do it super fast. How do they even make it?"

"There's…one distillery," Michaelis said, realizing what Noah meant. The palace would probably have to shell out emergency funds to get the distillery up to capacity.

"Lucky them," Noah said, and went back to monitoring metrics. Michaelis texted Alanna rather than Gregory; she said it was fine, that there was a *strategic Davzda reserve* that Gregory was going to empty out, and that there was a present on the way. He'd just received the text when a delivery driver knocked on the door.

"Your Grace," the woman said, with a bow that was made much more difficult by the enormous food package in her hands. "Compliments of the palace and Mr. Rambler, who said he'd come cook for you but he figured you'd like to celebrate in your own way."

Michaelis took the hamper from her, handing her a tip in return. "Thank you. Does he want a reply?"

"No sir. It's a very nice podcast, Your Grace," she added, seemingly on impulse. "The whole country's talking about it. We're trending again."

He smiled. "Lovely to hear. It's nice to be of service."

"Have a good evening," she said, and dashed back to her delivery van. Michaelis carried the hamper into the kitchen and opened it, texting a photograph to Eddie. The response came from Gregory – *You sounded great. Eddie and I are both very proud.*

It's only a podcast, he texted back.

Love you, was all he got in reply. He set the phone aside and began unpacking just as Jes and Noah emerged from downstairs.

"What's this?" Jes asked, leaning on the kitchen counter.

"Gifts from an admirer," he replied with a smile, setting out packets of meat wrapped in butcher's paper, a basket of new potatoes, and a box with what he suspected was a small cheesecake in it. "Gregory and Edward sent their regards and congratulations on the podcast."

"My admirers always sent flowers when I lived in New York," Jes said.

"Well, Americans, you know. No sense of substance," Michaelis replied, tossing a bag of cookies from the hamper to Noah. "Don't spoil your dinner too badly, I'll cook for you tonight. Oh, dear," he added, removing the last object in the hamper. It was a gray-green bottle of Davzda, but without the label. And he could see the mushrooms floating around in the bottom.

Jes whistled. "Well, now you have your very own illegal Davzda."

"Where the hell did Eddie Rambler dig this up?" Michaelis asked. "This is the real, old-school stuff with the mushrooms in it."

"Like an LSD cocktail," Jes agreed. "Do a shot or two of that and you'll think you've seen the divine."

"Don't even think about it," Michaelis told Noah, who was studying the mushrooms with interest. "I'm going to put this somewhere for very specific emergencies, possibly involving the end of the world."

"But you're cooking dinner?" Noah asked.

"Absolutely, as long as you're free," Michaelis said, glancing at Jes, who nodded. "Good. We'll have a celebration. We'll go boating and I'll catch us a few fish, so we'll have steak and fish on the grill."

He put away the various foodstuffs while Jes and Noah yelled to each other in their suite about what they were wearing and what they should bring. Noah wanted to bring his phone just to take photos with but Jes wanted him to get off the screen for a while; eventually they let him wear them down. Michaelis found a packet of dry rub in the hamper, so he prepared a pair of steaks and left them in the fridge to rest while he packed the potatoes in foil to be stuck into the coals, then fetched his bow and fishing kit from his room. By the time he'd changed into shabby old clothes for fishing and made sure he had what he needed, Noah was already preparing the boat at the dock.

Michaelis loaded bow and kit into the boat and made sure its ballasts were set properly; if you had to stand in a boat on open water and fire an arrow straight down into the lake, you generally wanted to make sure it was the most stable boat possible. He was just finishing up when Jes dropped lightly into the little craft, relaxing into the padded bench at the stern, aviator sunglasses slightly askew on their face. Michaelis felt a stab of affection that he hid by testing the draw on the bow.

"I can show you how, if you like," he said to Noah, who was undoing the mooring rope. "I taught Gregory when he was a little younger than you, but he'd studied archery in school."

"Can I just sit and watch and take videos?" Noah asked. "Promise I won't post them without showing them to you."

"I don't mind. Wouldn't be the first time. There's probably footage around from before you were even born," Michaelis said, kicking them off from the dock. "Right, if you're not going to fish, you row, how's that sound?"

"Where to, pal?" Noah asked, putting on what Michaelis imagined was a New York cabdriver's accent.

"Out that way, just shy of the middle of the lake," Michaelis said, pointing. "Then let the oars drop into the water."

Bowfishing was a Shivadh tradition, but it wasn't all that commonly practiced anymore; Michaelis was just a hobbyist, but he'd always enjoyed it. It used to be Miranda in the bow of the little boat, with Gregory in the stern curled up with a book or telling Michaelis all about the school year, while Michaelis at the oars basked in the presence of his family and waited until dusk for the fish to start to rise.

Now it was Jes in the stern, in a pair of baggy cargo shorts, wearing a t-shirt reading *Askazer-Shivadlakia* in a stylized sports logo font. They were sunning themself carelessly, one earbud in with the sound so low he couldn't even hear it in the silent stillness of the lake. Noah was between the oars, leaning over one side of the boat to study the clear water below. Not replacements; very different from his family, these two, and he couldn't think of them as his in the way he'd thought of his wife and son. But Noah had Gregory's studious curiosity and, like Gregory at fifteen, was all elbows and knees. And Jes...often made him feel the same way Miranda had, like there was a peace at his very core.

He examined the bow, making sure the wood wasn't cracked or brittle anywhere, as he considered this. It didn't occur to him for about ten minutes that the memory of Miranda hadn't hurt, not the way it often did.

"How long do you have to wait?" Noah whispered.

"Any minute now," Michaelis replied, drawing an arrow from the quiver in the bottom of the boat. He got to his feet slowly, adjusting to the gentle rocking of the boat, and took a handful of crumbs from his pocket, sprinkling them on the barely-rippling water. He heard the soft click of Noah's phone recording him.

"The trick of this," he said quietly, nocking the arrow and drawing it back, "is patience, but also endurance. You can't draw the bow when you see the fish – it's got to be before they rise, because otherwise when you do, the boat will rock and scare them off. Can't skip arm day," he added with a smile, repeating something Eddie had observed when he was learning.

"How long can you hold a bow like that?" Noah asked.

Michaelis saw a trout rise, hugely fat from summer feeding, and loosed the arrow before he thought about it. It hit the water with a resounding thwack, and the fish floated up to the surface, speared neatly on the shaft.

"Long enough," he said with a satisfied look, reaching down to shake it into the bucket. The arrow was wet, but didn't seem to have any damage, so he nocked it again.

"I always thought it was pretty medieval," Jes said.

"In a bad way?" Noah asked, still filming Michaelis, who

followed a shadow with the arrow for a while until he realized it was a piece of plant floating past.

"No, it just seemed kind of pointless," Jes said. Michaelis caught their eyes flicking over his arms, bare up to the cuffs of the t-shirt. "Very compelling in person, though."

"Shush," he murmured. "You two talkers are scaring off the fish."

Noah fell obediently silent, and Jes just looked at him over the top of their sunglasses. Michaelis ignored it, focusing on the water, flinching but not firing when a skater-bug skimmed past. After a few minutes he eased the bow down and took another handful of crumbs, scattering them slowly.

The fish burst to the surface, five or six of them flailing up at once as they sometimes did. He quickly nocked the arrow and fired, and then from habit held out his hand. He'd taught Gregory to pass him fresh arrows, but Gregory of course wasn't here – and yet an arrow slapped into his palm anyway. He drew and fired a second time, and a third when Noah passed him another one. Three fish, two neatly speared and one clearly shot but missing its arrow, floated up.

Michaelis crouched and set the bow down, pulling the fish into the bucket.

"That was very helpful," he said to Noah. "How did you know to hand them to me?"

"Just made sense," Noah said, shrugging.

"Well, you've earned your stripes today," Michaelis told him. Noah preened. "Mind rowing us back? I want to clean off the arrows and stretch my shoulders."

"You got it," Noah said, bringing them around with an expertise that said he'd probably been out in the boat, alone, when Jes and Michaelis weren't looking. Well, let the kid have a few secrets. That was part of growing up. He'd done it himself, fifty years ago.

At the dock, he let Noah tie up while he set the gear on the boards; Jes climbed out gracefully, and then instead of moving aside so he could join them, leaned back down and offered him their hand. He cocked an eyebrow at them, then took it and let them hand him out of the boat, not really stabilizing or lifting him, but very charming nonetheless.

"That's usually my job," he said.

"Gender roles are for wimps," they replied. Michaelis laughed. "Come on. Isn't it nice to have someone help you out for once?"

"Seems that's all anyone does these days, but yes," he agreed. "I'll clean the fish."

"My chivalry definitely does not extend to gutting fish," they agreed. Noah was already taking the gear back up to the lodge.

"Noah, bring the steaks on the plate in the fridge, please," Michaelis called, and Noah nodded. He caught Jes smiling at him sideways, and smiled sideways back, well pleased with the world.

It was a pretty good day, Jes had to admit. Michaelis might not want to pay attention to it, but the podcast was a success by first-episode standards and the buzz was pulling in a few listeners to the other shows as well. They'd had a light day of work, they'd gotten to watch Michaelis flex his arms and shoulders for whole minutes together, and there was surf and turf in their future. They stood at the grill and gathered up chunks of charcoal from the nearby bag, building the fire carefully to burn hot and fast at first.

Nearby, Michaelis was at a very elderly outdoor sink, showing Noah how to clean the fish. Out of deference to Noah's cries of "super gross" he was cutting one of them down to filets for the city child, but he left the heads and skin on the others, the better to grill them Shivadh-style. Jes hoped one of those was for them.

They stuck the potatoes right in among the coals as soon as possible – those would take a while to cook. They raked coals to one side to make a slightly cooler area for the meat just as Michaelis brought it over.

"It's all yours," they said, gesturing with the tongs. He accepted the tool with a nod and set to work. Jes retreated to the line of low-slung beach lounge chairs nearby.

"If you want to go swim, Noah, this won't be ready for a while," Michaelis called. Jes didn't even hear a response, just a shriek and the splash of a teenager cannonballing into the lake. "He's taking well to country life."

"He still thinks it's a treat," Jes said. "Normally he only gets this kind of outdoorsiness when we visit here."

"Do you suppose he misses the city?"

"He hasn't said he does. It's a lot quieter here after New York, but you know how kids get jaded when they grow up somewhere," Jes replied.

"And what about you?"

"Who's the interviewer now?" Jes asked, laughing. "Well, yes, there are some things I miss – delivery pizza, for one – but surprisingly not as much as I thought. I mean, New York will still be there if I want to go see it. This place is better for us now."

"I'm glad to hear it," Michaelis said.

"Were you concerned I'd be leaving once the podcast about the country is done?" Jes asked.

"No, that wasn't why I asked," Michaelis replied, leaving the food to cook while he washed his hands at the sink. "I remember enough from the question game to know there's also a good reason you are here in this country. Just wondering what you had to give up to come back."

"Not as much as you'd think. I do like it here. When I left, I just wanted out. What kid doesn't want to kick their hometown off their heels and see the world? I might have kicked a little harder than necessary, but in my defense my parents really needed a kicking. I left because of them. I came back for myself."

"I can't claim to know how you feel, given I literally took my father's job from him and then gave it to my son, but I know it can be difficult."

"Remember when you came to the studio and I got salty with you about being hereditary king in everything but name?"

"Faintly, yes," he said sardonically.

"I know you had a legitimate election, and I think you probably had a great reign, which I missed most of," Jes said. "But I am also still very mad at people who get to have the kind of good relationship with their dad that you had."

"Ah." Michaelis nodded. "If it's any consolation, you've done a great job with Noah. Easy to tell."

"Well, he's a good kid," Jes said.

"Hope he's a hungry one too," Michaelis replied, turning back to check on the food. Jes lay in the sun-dappled shade under the tree cover and let themself drift, enjoying the quiet and the smell of charcoal, and Noah's occasional shouts from the lake.

"All right, this fish is almost overdone and the steak's pink," Michaelis said eventually, nudging their chair with his foot. "Noah! Dinner!"

"Coming!" Noah called, and ran up the dock, ducking under the outdoor shower head near the sink to rinse off. Jes got up to wash their hands and then took the platter of meat from Michaelis, who followed with the potatoes. As they settled in at the table, Jes realized what they were seeing in him – the same brightness he showed whenever Gregory was in the room. It was like the real Michaelis was emerging from a thin, dark shell. If this was what he'd been like as king, no wonder he'd been good at his job. He was always kind and usually fun, but this Michaelis was charming as well.

He wasn't a bad cook, either, they thought, as he put one of the head-on fish on their plate and served the filets, with deep grill marks and crisp brown edges, to Noah. Jes ate eagerly, savoring something that tasted like the best parts of their childhood.

"Michaelis," Noah said, phone set into a little portable tripod and filming him, "how do they make Davzda, anyway? The real stuff that's not legal."

Michaelis set his fork down, clearing his throat. "I suppose it's like absinthe. You start with spirits – if you post this, you should put a disclaimer that this is not a recipe," he said abruptly.

"Promise," Noah said.

"There's a mildly hallucinogenic mushroom that used to grow – and does not anymore, so visitors please don't go pulling up mushrooms on your hikes – in the highlands," Michaelis continued. "The mushrooms would be dried in hot salt. They become very salty, obviously. Then you'd add a couple of those to a bottle and fill it with distilled spirits – which was usually home-made to begin with, so it's always been difficult to gauge the alcohol content. Some people add other spices if they want their drink to taste like, I don't know, regret and cloves instead of just regret. The hallucinogen leeches into the alcohol as the mushrooms rehydrate, so if you shake up the bottle first, you get a little high on top of the alcohol when you drink."

"What if you don't shake the bottle?"

"Then the last person to drink has quite the time."

"Did you ever drink the real stuff?" Noah asked.

"Not intentionally. Once when I was very young and making poor choices in friends."

"But was it fun?" Noah asked, grinning.

Michaelis smiled. "Eat your fish, Noah. You can make your own mistakes when you're older."

Michaelis had learned, somewhat recently if he was honest, that when something was going right, when things were swimming in his direction, he shouldn't question his instincts or feelings. He'd always been analytical, a good quality in a leader, but retirement had meant a readjustment in his thought processes.

He'd been pleased with the gift from the king – still novel and amusing to think of Gregory as the king – and he'd enjoyed boating and fishing, and tending the food. Building the fire was always the part he'd disliked, and Jes had simply gone to do it without even mentioning it, which was gratifying. Dinner was both good and celebratory.

Now, full from dinner and laid out in one of the lounge chairs, with Jes in the one next to his and Noah dutifully clearing the table, he refused to question why he felt so happy or what he could do to hold onto it. Instinct would tell him, and questioning things would only shorten the pleasure of them. Instead he simply folded his hands over his stomach, shoulders twinging pleasantly, and contemplated the lake until his eyelids drooped.

He was more than half-asleep when he felt a soft touch, fingertips ruffling his short hair. The pressure against his scalp felt good and for a second he leaned into it, until he realized he wasn't sure who was doing it, and then he startled awake.

The touch vanished. He sat halfway up, turning; Jes was still in the next chair over, lying on their side facing him, their hand hovering in the air, looking stricken.

"I'm sorry," they said. "I should have asked first, you just had a leaf on your hair, and it's softer than I expected – "

"No, it's fine," he said. "I was almost asleep. I wasn't sure where I was for a moment."

"Ah. Still. I know better," they said, giving him an only slightly brittle smile. He cast around for how to say that he'd liked it, and then felt stupid for a split second.

"It was nice," he said. "Just unexpected. I liked it. I'm not accustomed to, uh. Touch."

He glanced at their hand, still in midair, and then back at their face; they saw the look and hovered their hand closer. He nodded and laid back, eyes open now; they skimmed their fingers through his hair, brushing against the grain, sending tingles down his scalp.

"I was a kid, but I remember there was an absolute scandal

when you cut your hair right after the coronation," they said, after a few moments of absent stroking. He closed his eyes. "My mother said you looked like a shorn lamb."

"The seventies were over," he replied. "Time to be a king."

"Was that why?"

"Honestly? I had to wear the crown a lot, at the start," he said. Their fingers dug into his temple before moving back to the tense muscles just behind his ear. "Hair kept getting caught in it."

"Ever practical," they replied. "It does get a little lonely out here. I can see how an unexpected touch might startle you. Every morning when Lachlan gets here I make him give me a hug just so I don't get out of practice."

"Well, you can do this whenever you like," Michaelis murmured. "Feels fantastic."

"Might take you up on that. Or I might make you cook me fish that good again, as a tax."

"I saw you coveting the heads."

"Noah thinks it's weird. He always has. I don't know, you try to raise them in all the old ways…"

Michaelis chuckled. Jes's fingers dug into the crown of his head, blunt nails creating sharp just-this-side-of-pain pressure before they spread their fingers wider.

"Sleep if you want," they said. "It's only me and Noah here."

He nodded against the touch and closed his eyes, but he stayed awake for a while, the better to enjoy it. He felt a little guilty, but he couldn't bring himself to care; their fingers were warm and soothing, pressing out knots of tension and scrubbing at the base of his skull. When they finally flattened their palm on the crown of his head again, then left it there, he slipped into sleep.

Jes could tell the moment Michaelis slept; the muscles in his jaw went lax, and the last lines of tension around his eyes smoothed out. They left their hand on his head, resting on the short silver hair, watching him sleep.

It wasn't exactly that the idea of the king as a man was foreign to them; Askazer-Shivadlakia was a small place and the Shivadh people weren't overawed by their rulers even before they started voting for them. Living with him certainly humanized him too. But when they were a kid the king was a more distant figure, and every time they were reminded he was human it amused them.

Michaelis had a healthy respect for Davzda until he'd had a few shots of it. He was a tidy man. He liked the outdoors; he was a runner and swimmer, a bowfisher. It was clear he'd spent as much time worrying about his parenting as Jes currently was. He smiled quick and sharp, the way he did many things. He had a startle reflex, and he liked having his scalp rubbed.

They really shouldn't have done it without asking, but he didn't seem like someone who had a particularly high guard against such things. At least he hadn't been angry, just confused.

He wasn't one of Jes's friends back in New York, always hugging and casually touching, sitting hip-to-hip on sofas, dancing close in clubs. He was a widower with an adult son and not much to occupy his time, and nobody much to touch him.

They sat back and picked up their book, reading while Michaelis breathed softly and slowly in the next chair. Noah finished cleaning up and went back down to the dock, this time to sit on it and pitch pebbles into the water.

Well, Michaelis didn't have anyone to touch him and Jes wanted more touch; there was an obvious solution there, and they watched Noah skip stones and strategized about it. Michaelis was obliging when he saw someone with a need, much less stubborn than he would be if he was faced with an offer of help. He could see sense, and he didn't seem particularly averse to touch, just surprised by it.

The sun was just barely down when they got out of the chair and nudged Michaelis awake.

"Noah snitched that there's a cheesecake inside," they said. "Noah, come on, dessert."

Inside the lodge, Jes sliced up the cheesecake and distributed plates. While they ate, Noah showed Michaelis how he was editing the fishing video to make it look more professional.

"Okay, I'm gonna go look at the metrics and do some stuff," Noah announced at last.

"Please, I am begging you to be a normal child and play a video game," Jes said.

"If you insist," Noah said, in such an obvious imitation of Michaelis at his most dignified that even Michaelis laughed.

"I'll be out here for a while. Put yourself to bed when you get tired and remember to brush your teeth," Jes said. "Goodnight, love you," they sing-songed, and Noah chimed in on the last few syllables. Michaelis took their plates to the sink and stretched.

"I should probably turn in," he said.

"Come, sit for a little while," Jes told him, heading into the living room. He followed, then grinned as they grasped his shoulders and maneuvered him to the sofa, settling him on the cushions not quite next to one arm. He looked a little surprised when they dropped down next to him, back to the arm of the sofa, swinging their legs up to prop over his lap, but he didn't object.

"Keep me company," Jes commanded, placing a book from the side-table in his hands.

"What are you doing?" he asked, but he propped the book open on their knees.

"Sitting with you. Reading," they replied. "Objections?"

"Not materially, just curious."

They leaned their head against the back of the sofa. "I told you I miss all the hugs I used to get, and I thought maybe you'd like sitting here too. Seemed like you were a little starved for touch this afternoon."

"I do fine," he replied, looking down at the book.

"I'm sure you do, but fine is only adequate. Anyway it's not about you, egotist. When I was twenty I'd have gone clubbing to celebrate something like this. Might have thrown a huge dinner party when I was thirty-five." They nudged his chest with their knee. "At forty-five, what I want is someone else to cook me dinner and then keep me company while I read."

"Let me tell you, at sixty all you ever want is a nap," he said, settling in. Keeping his right hand on the book, he rubbed his jaw with his left, and then very deliberately rested it on Jes's ankle, propped next to his thigh. His palm was warm on the top of their bare foot, thumb cupped around the curve of their leg.

Jes took out their cellphone and scrolled through the news app, looking for anything interesting or timely for the podcast. For a while there was just the soft noise of his book's pages turning, and the faint, distant rumble of whatever shoot-em-up game Noah was playing.

Eventually, Michaelis's hand twitched; Jes watched as his thumb swept up their ankle and then back down, an absent soothing movement. Still engrossed in his book, he did it again, and then settled into a slow rhythm with it, apparently unaware he was doing it. It felt wonderful – intimate in a weird, Victorian way, the touch of a hand on an ankle, but also innocent. Nothing meant by it, nothing demanded. He was simply comfortable enough to touch them.

He kept it up until at last he yawned, raising his hand to cover his mouth, and set the book aside.

"Bed?" Jes asked.

"Mm." He leaned back to let them lift their legs up, then slid out from under them, stretching as he stood. "Thank you. Sleep well."

"You too," they said, and watched him go, admiring the lines of his shoulders through his shirt. Well, one could dream, and in the meantime perhaps they could help each other.

Perhaps he might want them both to stay here in the fall, and if he did, Jes didn't see how they would be willing to say no.

The next morning, instead of lingering in the doorway as he usually did, Michaelis came into the kitchen while Jes was staring sleepily at the toaster, willing it to toast faster. He nudged them out of the way with a hand on their hip, helped himself to the still-brewing coffee, and then brushed their elbow with one hand to get their attention, passing them the jam.

Jes smiled to themself and, when he got in their way trying to scramble an egg, hip-checked him to make him move over.

Eddie had actually been a little hesitant to do a podcast with a kid, even a kid like Noah. He'd listened to *Echo Junior* enough to know that it was a fine show for teenagers and actually pretty smart, but one never knew how much of that was editing, or even Jes stage-parenting their son. He'd agreed easily when talking to Jes because he had a policy of never saying no to something unless he had to, but he'd had his doubts.

Emailing back and forth with Noah had put his mind at ease. Noah was a young professional, with release forms to sign and a very thorough explanation of what he could expect. Further, the kid was *fun* – he wanted Eddie to tell funny stories and give advice, not just talk about the tourist initiative or his thoughts on food trends. He'd asked, too, what Eddie thought would be a neat thing to do for the podcast.

Remembering Gregory's request to do a little casual spying, Eddie had said, "Why don't you interview me while I'm cooking? I could come cook dinner for the fam at the lodge, and you could record while I cook, then we'll do a roundtable while we eat."

He felt it was working out exceptionally well. He'd arrived with groceries and a couple of recipes in mind to find Noah and Lachlan already set up with recording equipment – a wireless mic for him, stationary mics at the stove and cutting board to record ambient cooking noises, and thick quilts temporarily stapled to the walls to muffle echoes.

Michaelis and Jes were meant to be two of the dinner guests, he knew, but perhaps out of respect for Noah's creative process they didn't show up until the meal was ready. Jes opened and poured the wine while Michaelis, former king, diplomat, and imposing son of a bitch, set the table. Eddie's mind was a little blown by the image.

"How did the interview go?" Michaelis asked, as they settled in to eat.

"Really well, I think," Eddie said, and Noah, mouth already full of goat "Askazer Style," nodded agreement. "I love talking while I cook. My very first cooking show was this dumb little cable access thing I did in college," he added, helping himself to some bread. "It was just me and a camera in a corner of a dorm kitchen, and I used to lock everyone out so I could film. Which turned out to be a huge mistake. I don't know if you know this about me – I'm sure His Grace knows and would agree – but I am a people person."

"I'd venture to say you are the most people person I've met in a long career in politics," Michaelis added drily.

"So the show sucked," Eddie said. "Because I didn't have anyone to talk to. No outlet for my natural charm. One day I forgot to lock the door and a couple of guys walked in and just kinda – stared at me and I stared at them, and then I said well, you're here, you want some tacos?"

"Nobody ever says no to tacos," Noah said.

"You are correct. And that particular video got super popular on campus because it was funny. Because I had an audience, someone for the viewer at home to identify with. It went into my audition reel when I got my big break at Eat Network."

"You learned to play to your strengths," Jes said.

"Yes, but also to recognize what they were. Sometimes we're the only ones who know that what we're good at is worthwhile. Like, you gotta value what you do, or else why do it?" Eddie asked.

"Why wouldn't people value being friendly?" Noah asked.

"Oh, the usual damaged reasons. You're not cool enough, you're too nice, you talk about stuff nobody cares about," Eddie said. "Nuts. That's just people who are afraid to make friends."

"It's a very good strategy," Michaelis said. "Difficult to execute sometimes, but wise to have as an option. Being… unexpectedly transparent. Sincere."

"Yeah. Though sometimes in show business you do just have to pretend to be real cool until they're not looking," Eddie agreed.

He let his mouth run without paying too much attention to it, a skill he'd cultivated over years of interviews. He wanted to stay engaged with the podcast but he was also watching a fascinating silent dynamic play out around the dinner table, and a part of his mind was distracted trying to figure it out.

For a start, this wasn't the dry, slightly cutting Michaelis he was accustomed to, a man who strode through life efficiently and without much pause for other peoples' opinions. He seemed calmer – he might have objected to the word, but Eddie thought perhaps even *softer*. Gregory had been right, there was a change, and it was particularly visible at the dining table of the lodge, in the company of friends.

Or, perhaps, in the company of Jes Deimos. They were seated next to Michaelis, frequently stealing vegetables off his plate, which he had apparently rotated specifically so they could. Michaelis watched Jes when they spoke, and when he spoke to Noah he occasionally glanced at Jes as if he wanted to be sure what he was saying to their kid was okay. It must be an awkward form of quasi-co-parenting, living with a precocious kid like Noah but not being officially any kind of dad.

When Eddie finished the story he'd been telling, Lachlan cleared his throat and turned his laptop to face them. Poor man was eating off his lap while he continued to keep the sound going – Eddie made a note to leave him a special helping of dessert.

"Found the video online," Lachlan said. Eddie's twenty-one-year-old baby face, under a pile of disorderly blue hair, stared out at them blurrily.

"Oh, wow," Eddie laughed. "There I am, making tacos for nobody. About fifteen seconds from now – yeah, hit play – there I go, there's the deer in the headlights," he said, as the onscreen Eddie froze in the middle of assembling a taco. Two figures were standing in front of the right side of the camera, out of focus.

"Oh hey," Eddie on the video said. "You guys look super high. You want some tacos?"

Lachlan was grinning over the edge of the laptop; Noah and Jes were both laughing, and Michaelis's chuckle was a deep rumble underneath. Eddie glanced over in time to see Jes wipe a tear of laughter from the corner of their eye and glance at Michaelis, affection and delight in their look. Perhaps they'd been concerned about him too, as the palace had been. They seemed happy to see him laughing.

"I forgot I told them they looked high," Eddie said, as Lachlan closed the window and went back to work. "Wasn't wrong, though. I know because the tacos weren't nearly as good as they said they were."

The rest of dinner went fine, but he was still chewing over what he'd seen when he arrived back at the palace, making his way up to Gregory's rooms. The king was on the sofa, for once without the requisite pile of spreadsheets or diplomatic reports, reading a graphic novel that one of Eddie's brothers had sent him in their last package. Eddie dropped down next to him and flopped dramatically against his shoulder. Gregory absently rested his chin on Eddie's head.

"Interview go well?" he asked, setting the book aside.

"Yeah, and the goat came out nicely too," Eddie said.

"Well, what's really important here?"

"Making goat edible is important," Eddie informed him. "Anyway, Noah had a good time and I think he got some strong audio, and he and I talked about getting the podcast network some publicity."

"Don't work yourself too hard," Gregory said.

"This is my favorite kind of work, after cooking," Eddie said. "It'll be fine, I'll roll it into some other stuff I'm doing. And your dad and Jes had a good time, I think."

"Oh yes?" Gregory said.

"Yeah. I know you were curious, and it's not like I could go through his underwear drawer or something – "

"I didn't want you to take it that far," Gregory said.

"But he seemed content. You know how you said it was weird to see him so happy? I think what's weird is just…seeing a change in someone. Maybe you got used to him being unhappy."

"That's possible," Gregory admitted. "I told you when you came here that he wasn't at his best."

"I remember. I think he's good now, though," Eddie said. "I think he's enjoying having people to look after. Maybe people who look after him. Hard for him to do that with you right now, you know? Maybe he missed it."

"I suppose," Gregory said. "But he's all right, you think?"

"Yes. I don't think you need to worry about him," Eddie said. He kept his thoughts about the way Jes and Michaelis looked at each other to himself, for now.

CHAPTER EIGHT

ONCE THE FIRST episode of the podcast came out, it felt like something locked into a rhythm – like a clean shot with a bow, or a gear shifting correctly in a car.

Michaelis spent most of his mornings now in the library, happy to be back with a good purpose. He spoke with the librarian about writing the boring parts of his memoirs down and doing the podcast on the interesting ones, and the man gave him a relieved look and permission to go ahead. In the afternoons, he recorded with Noah or Jes, or he worked on scripts – mostly his own, but sometimes looking at Noah's as well, helping with grammar or pointing out what wasn't clear. He broke his own rule about not reading his reviews and read the comments on his episodes, looking for ways to improve, relieved that he was apparently too old to take any of the uglier criticism personally. They all just came off so childish, like toddlers clamoring for attention.

Often, in the evenings, he or Jes would find each other and settle in on the sofa to read, or to exchange dry looks while Noah watched reality television.

"Gregory has an invitation for us," he said one evening, studying his phone while Jes and Noah bickered about what was on television.

"Us?" Jes asked, curious.

"Eddie's been trying out the surfing all along the coast, and he thinks he's found the best spot. He and Gregory are doing a little video thing for the Photogram this week of the two of them surfing. He wants to know if I'd like to come along, and you both as well. He says he struck a deal with Noah about publicity."

"Noah?" Jes prompted.

"Professional dealings, confidential," Noah said with a grin. "Eddie just said after the interview that he thought we should have a higher profile. He said he'd find some opportunities. We're paying him in studio time at some future date."

"Savvy, that one," Michaelis murmured. "Well, I wouldn't mind a trip to the beach, but if Eddie's been there it'll be full of tourists and Photogram models."

Noah looked like he was actually excited about the idea of a beach full of Photogram models, which was when Michaelis remembered that Noah was fifteen, and the vast majority of the Photogram models in Askazer-Shivadlakia at the moment were teenage girls from Italy and France who found boys with American accents extra-interesting.

"Can we, Boss?" Noah asked. "It'd be rude to turn down an invitation from the king, right?"

"Entirely up to you," Michaelis said to Jes. "If you'd like, I can just take Noah."

Jes gave him a sweeping look, and Michaelis wondered if they were considering all the times he'd come in from swimming without a shirt on.

"No, we'll both go, and please thank Gregory for the invite," they decided. "But you, Wild Child, have to promise you will put sunscreen on every single time I tell you, and you, Your Grace," they kicked him gently, "have to keep him in eyeshot. No letting him wander off to canoodle with the Photogrammers."

Spotted in the sun: King Gregory III of Askazer-Shivadlakia takes a break from politics to hit the waves with his boyfriend, influencer and celebrity chef Eddie Rambler. Video via Photogram.

Askazer-Shivadlakia is this summer's hottest and hardest to pronounce ticket thanks to Eddie Rambler, who spread the country's fame among his hip social media following during the king's recent coronation. While movie stars and tech moguls sun themselves in Monaco, the young, the broke, and the photogenic have made tracks for this tiny beachfront country, to fill your feed with sun-kissed smiles, quaint cafes, beautiful vistas, and friendly local color.

Also at the beach to watch the king wipe out was his father, His Grace King Emeritus Michaelis, along with GenX nerd idol Jes Deimos, who chatted with a steady stream of Photogram influencers and podcast fans. Deimos's son Noah, an influencer in his own right, stuck close to the royal family and eventually gave up his phone to catch some sun with a beach read. The Deimos family is working with the royals to produce a series of podcasts about life in "The Ask".

"I can hear my father bellowing from this side of the veil," Michaelis said at palace breakfast, when he saw the puff piece on their beach trip. *"They call my country The Ask? They call the country of the Askazer warrior and the Shivadh noble The ASK?"*

"Grandfather did love a good bellow," Gregory agreed.

"So strange he didn't pass it on," Jerry said, with a grin at Michaelis.

"There's a time and place for yelling. If you knew it, you'd be king instead of that one," Michaelis said, pointing at Gregory.

"Want me to put the kibosh on?" Eddie asked around a mouthful of breakfast. "It's a hashtag on Photogram but I can slap that shit down and make them thank me for it. If I can learn to say Askazer-Shivadlakia, these idiots can."

"The tourism office might have input on that," Alanna said.

"I say this as advice, not command, but if you let them brand us as The Ask your ancestors will curse us," Michaelis said, and Jerry cackled with laughter.

"I have to say, Greg, it's a great picture of you," he continued. "Uncle Mike looks fantastic too."

"I didn't see a picture of me," Michaelis said, frowning.

"Down at the bottom, here." Jerry passed him his phone.

It was a fairly flattering photo – Jes was actually the focus, barefoot in the sand in their vintage-style one piece, watching Gregory surf. Michaelis was just behind them and to one side, wearing Gregory's spare rash guard and a pair of plain blue swim trunks, damp hair ruffled up in a cowlick like he'd always had when he was younger.

"Look at you, fashion model," Alanna said, nudging Michaelis gently.

Michaelis nodded absently, studying the picture. He did look nice, and unless someone was looking very closely or projecting very hard, they wouldn't see that his eyes were on Jes, and the smile on his face was more affectionate than was proper. He was the widower king emeritus, after all, and Jes could have their pick of people, outside of a difficult curmudgeon they'd accidentally charmed.

"Could you send me the image, Jerry? I don't know how to do the little picture doodad," he said. He did know how, but complaining and making Jerry do it was a form of entertainment.

"Actually, that's a pretty good quote, Your Grace," Alanna said. "The country of the Askazer warrior and the Shivadh noble. Is that from a book, or did you make that up?"

"It's just something like my father would say," Michaelis replied. "If you quote me don't say warrior, I don't like that to represent Askaz. Say scholar. Or say Askazer poet and Shivadh scholar, that rolls off the tongue better and it's no less true."

"The people of Askazer-Shivadlakia are poet scholar warrior

philosopher kings," Gregory said to Eddie. "We think somewhat highly of ourselves."

"Ain't bragging if it's true," Eddie said. "Learned that from bumper stickers in truck stops all the way across Texas. Anyway, I'm glad Jes and Noah could come to the beach too. Those kids are going places."

"Isn't Jes about fifteen years older than you are?" Michaelis asked.

"I was born an old soul," Eddie replied.

"Save us from Californians," Michaelis said.

"Tell you what, I wouldn't want to be on the wrong side of Jes Deimos," Jerry said. "Have you heard their podcast?"

Everyone looked at him.

"What?" Jerry asked.

"Father is *on* their podcast. Eddie's promoting them. The rest of us have been listening for months. What have you been doing?" Gregory asked.

"Making trouble," Jerry replied unconcernedly.

"For whom?" Michaelis inquired.

"Never you mind, Uncle Mike. The point is, there goes someone who could ravage you emotionally and destroy you professionally but also I want their skincare regimen," Jerry said. "If I were the settling-down type I'd propose."

"I'd dearly love to see that," Michaelis replied.

"Some day you're going to trip and fall for someone headlong, Jerry, and I hope I'm there when it happens," Alanna said sweetly. "Your Grace, I'll pass along your supernatural prognostication about The Ask to comms. Eddie?"

"Yep, let's go confab," Eddie said, rising to follow her out. "What if we didn't call it The Ask, but made that like a slogan. *We're here – Just Ask!*"

"You're not genuinely concerned, are you?" Gregory asked, as Jerry trailed after them to offer his own suggestions.

"I just think it's tacky, and not tacky in a good way, like

Eddie," Michaelis said. "The tourism is good for us but we can't let it be our guiding principle. At least, that's my opinion," he added conscientiously.

"I do value that, you know."

"As well you should," Michaelis said with a smile. "Any other dilemmas I can advise on?"

"Not at present. You've got your hands full, anyway."

"Yes, it's been pleasantly busy lately." Michaelis stood, tugging on his jacket. "I'll be in the library this morning, but probably not around for lunch. Recording early this afternoon and then Noah asked for some help with school preparations. He needs to get enrolled somewhere and apparently he has several options, so he wants my advice."

"The Highlands School is the most well-funded. Probably the best teaching overall," Gregory said.

"Yes, but it's a long trek up there on a daily basis, and Jes tells me Noah's schooling is something of a formality. He's an independent learner, as if that wasn't blindingly obvious. I suspect he needs patient teachers more than prestigious ones."

"Well, I'm sure he'll figure it out. Good luck," Gregory said. "There's always an opening at Institut Alpin, or can be if I write him a letter of recommendation."

"Hurrah for the old school!" Michaelis cried as he left.

"I don't see why school even matters," Noah said, when they sat down at the conference table in the bunker that afternoon to go over his options. Jes had a couple of shiny pamphlets from the local schools, and Noah had his laptop open to the websites. "You dropped out and you did fine."

"I did not do fine, I had to get a GED and then go back to school while working full time and it sucked," Jes said. "Let's try and avoid that for you."

"And you probably should at least know how trigonometry works, even if you forget the details as I clearly have," Michaelis said, studying Noah's previous school's transcripts. "The good news is you're a little ahead of most Shivadh students your age, so you can go into – what would Americans call it? Junior year? And have time to fit in without worrying about catching up."

"Yeah, as if that's ever happened," Noah muttered.

"It could happen now," Jes said gently. "You'll be the cool new kid at school."

"I just think I could learn this stuff faster on my own."

"And possibly you could," Michaelis agreed. "But school isn't just learning or socializing, it's an ongoing experience. It gives you something in common with other people. Which, if you want to stay in Askazer-Shivadlakia, will be important. You're a citizen, but that doesn't mean you know everything about living here yet."

"Learning a lot though," Noah said, rebellion still in his voice.

"All good points, but sometimes, kiddo, you just gotta jump through a few hoops in this life," Jes said wearily.

"Oh. Well. If it's just hoops," Noah replied. Michaelis glanced at Jes, wondering if it could be that easy. "Two years of jumping through hoops is a real pain in the butt, but if that's all it is, I can probably do that. As long as I still get to do the podcast and stuff."

"Thank goodness for small favors," Jes said. "Does this get you any closer to figuring out which one you want to go to?"

"Why do they start so late?" Noah asked. "Doesn't school normally start in September most places?"

"The olive harvest," Michaelis said. "Olive season is August and September, and children were needed at home to help. Not as many people farm olives now, but all the kids still go out to the groves, make a little extra pocket money. Most of the teachers work in the groves over the summers, too."

"Can I go do an olive harvest?" Noah asked Jes.

"Sure, you've got your youth worker's card," Jes said. "Do an episode on it. Or I will."

"Let's focus on getting you enrolled, so you at least have somewhere to go afterward," Michaelis said, trying to redirect both parent and child towards the pamphlets. "The Highlands School is arguably the best, but – "

"No, it's too far," Noah said.

"Well, of the ones close enough for you to attend day school and decent enough you should consider them, that leaves the Western Lowlands School, the Yeshiva, and this strange place down by the harbor in Fons-Askaz where you spend one day a week on a tall ship," Michaelis said, picking up the pamphlet for the Maritime Academy. "I should have paid more attention to our accrediting board when I was king."

"It looks like a military school but it's not," Noah said. "The messageboards say it's actually pretty cool. You can set a lot of your own curriculum once you pass the basics and I can test out of most of them. And it's close."

"Very snappy uniforms," Jes said.

"Don't love uniforms on the whole," Noah replied dubiously. "But they are unisex, so I have to give them that. I could go to school in a kilt."

"I'm fond of them," Jes replied. "You ever wear a kilt, Michaelis?"

"Too much of a breeze for me," Michaelis said. "Does come with a handy place for storing one's wallet and keys, though. I can't recommend the Yeshiva unless you want to be a rabbi, but the best I can say of the Western Lowlands School is that it's…adequate."

"Snob," Jes told him. "He went to boarding school," they said to Noah.

"Really?"

Michaelis nodded absently. "Institut Alpin. It's called the school of kings, but not on my account. Lots of powerful peoples' children are educated there. It's in the Swiss Alps, very cold in the winter. I loved it. Gregory tolerated it well. It's a great education, but not, I think, for you."

"Why not? Other than the obvious, that it's a Swiss boarding school like something out of an 80s movie about an evil stepmother," Noah said.

"It's very structured and traditional. They would try to train you for a life I don't think you want," Michaelis said. "If you want to go into hedge fund management or high civil service – "

"Blegh. No offense."

"None taken. I always told Gregory, you have to want the job," Michaelis said. "I did, he did. You, young broadcast journalist, do not. Are you thinking of journalism school?"

Noah glanced at Jes, who shrugged. "Don't ask me, kid, it's your life. I can advise, but I can't pick it out for you."

"What if I don't know?" Noah asked.

Michaelis considered it. He'd known pretty young, and Gregory had too. If he hadn't known, he definitely wouldn't have gone to Institut Alpin, as much as he'd liked it there.

"If you aren't working directly towards a goal yet," he said slowly, "then there's no point going somewhere that's going to try to push you towards one you might not want. You should...explore, I suppose. Like your parent did – learn what's out there in the world. In a structured way through formal education, and not by running off to another country," he added, when he saw Jes's look.

"Huh." Noah sifted through the pamphlets again. "It'd be cool to learn, like, knot tying and sailing and stuff. And useful, I guess. I could get credit for the podcast."

"Sounds like the Maritime Academy would be a fine choice, then," Michaelis said.

"Anyway, most schools are pretty much the same, aren't they?" Noah continued. "Reading, writing, arithmetic. College prep, school dances."

"I suppose in some respects, but not all. I had to take comportment at boarding school, and they still taught it when Gregory went," Michaelis said.

"Comportment?" Noah asked, grinning.

"Of course. Manners, dancing, table etiquette, how to address nobility. All of that. A good skill set for a king to have."

"What kind of dancing? I mean, I guess not like...Photogram dances," Noah said.

"No," Michaelis laughed. "More like *Strictly Come Dancing*. Ballroom," he clarified. "I've probably spent more time waltzing than you've spent alive."

"Funny to think of you dancing," Jes said.

"Why?" Michaelis asked.

"I don't know, I suppose I think of the king as the guy who sits on the throne and watches others dance."

"Great opportunity for diplomacy, dancing. Everyone should know a little," Michaelis said. "And a waltz is easy, so you can talk and dance at the same time."

"It never looks easy on the dancing shows," Noah said.

"Of course not, they want you caught up in the drama of it all. Here, I'll show you." Michaelis took out his phone, scrolling through his playlist for a waltz and putting it on, the music low. He stood up and offered Noah a hand. "I'll teach you how, it doesn't take long."

"Ginger Rogers did everything Fred Astaire did, backwards and in heels," Jes said.

"Yes, I have seen that t-shirt," Michaelis informed them. Noah narrowed his eyes at Michaelis, but got up and took his hand. "Now. As your parent says, generally the lady has to dance backwards, but in Askazer-Shivadlakia, if she's of higher rank than you, you have to. And what if you have two men dancing, like now? Or if you're dancing with someone like Jes? A gentleman, Noah, always knows both parts, and defers to his partner's preference."

"Doesn't sound like much fun, being a gentleman," Noah said, as Michaelis positioned them on the open floor.

"I've always enjoyed the gallantry aspect of it," Jes said. "Getting to make someone feel special. That transcends gender."

"Or it ought," Michaelis agreed. "All right, so if you lead, we do a simple box step…"

Noah was a quick study, as Michaelis had expected, but he didn't seem particularly enthusiastic about it. Which was fair; unless you were training to be king, he supposed it wasn't a very relevant life skill a lot of the time. After teaching him to lead and at least to know when he was following, he let Noah go back to the table, idly paging through the Maritime Academy pamphlet again.

"Here, kid, let me show you how it's done," Jes said, getting up. Before Michaelis could come up with either an excuse or a good reason they shouldn't, Jes had placed one hand in Michaelis's and the other under his arm, in the leading position.

"Sure you're up for this?" Michaelis managed. "I've done this a lot more often than you have."

"That's cute, but drag and ballroom dancing are like half an inch apart," Jes said. "I've waltzed with men in heels higher than your opinion of yourself right now."

"Burn," Noah commented, sitting back to watch.

"Noah, turn Michaelis's old-dude music off and get my phone," Jes said, giving Michaelis a narrow look. "Track two on the dance beat playlist."

"Oooh," Noah said, queuing up some fancy pop song Michaelis wasn't familiar with.

"Quickstep," Jes told Michaelis, and about half a second later swept him off his feet.

He knew how to dance, that was automatic, and he could do a quickstep while following, but Jes had a bounce to them that he barely kept up with, and they were less cautious about banging into the furniture than he was. It took a few bars to get his feet truly under him, but then it was – well, fun, swinging around the room, letting Jes direct the movement, keeping his focus on their face to keep from getting dizzy. Noah was singing along to the song in the background, and when it went to a typical pop-music bridge, Jes spun around and said, "Okay, now you."

He jumped into the lead role, keeping their orbit a little tighter just in case they'd been straying near furniture, and for the last minute of the song was really only paying attention to Jes, not even to the music or Noah or the room spinning behind them.

When the music ended, they swirled to a stop and Michaelis stepped back and bowed. Jes lifted his hand in theirs and kissed the back of it, grinning. It felt like an electric shock ran through his body.

"Okay, that was a little cool," Noah said, somewhere in the distance.

"Thanks," Jes said, turning away to sit down again.

Michaelis stood there for a moment, startled and confused, lit up with a desire he hadn't even thought he was capable of anymore.

Jes was fun and interesting and had flirted before, but that had just been entertaining, nothing expected to come from it. Now – very abruptly – he *wanted.*

"Getting your breath back?" Jes asked from the table, where they'd settled back in with Noah.

"Ah, yes. And some water, I think. Anything for you?" he asked, going to the sink to compose himself. It wasn't entirely successful, but at least it put some distance between him and that dance.

"No, I'm good," Jes replied. "Thanks, that was fun."

He had to get his breathing, and his pulse, and his damn emotions all under control. This wasn't an accidental affectionate look at the beach, this was bound to be obvious. He took down a glass, slowly, and filled it with water. By the time he'd downed half of it, his body at least was settled back into itself.

He came back to the table, sitting across from Noah, who was chattering at Jes about enrolling and school supplies and uniforms. All very familial. Like Noah was a second son, blithely unworried about the crown.

This was...this was probably unwise. Not just his being here, pretending at parenthood of a child that wasn't his, but this sudden, sharp, bewildering attraction. He couldn't act on it. Jes lived here, they were working together, and – he'd spent his whole life with women, well, with a single specific woman, who he was well aware he was not entirely over and probably never would be. Unfair to Jes. And he had no idea how to go about navigating anything more complicated than he already had with Jes.

But he wanted to. He wanted to learn how to. Also unfair to make Jes show him.

He considered this while Jes and Noah battled their way through the paperwork. If this was just his libido waking up after a few years of grieving, it could go right back to sleep. He wouldn't hurt Jes that way simply because they were present and available and possibly even amenable. He'd enjoyed knowing they thought he was attractive, noticing it and encouraging it, when he knew neither of them wanted it to go anywhere.

Now his mind whispered that there were all kinds of places it could go. Some of them were thrilling. Not all of them were good.

Well, that was what research was for, he supposed. He liked books, but he'd be at sea trying to find books about this. Jes, on the other hand, liked people – going to first-hand sources, finding experts, talking to witnesses.

He leaned forward briefly to pick his phone up off the table, pulling up his text messages.

Word with you tomorrow? he asked Gregory, not expecting a swift reply, but one came back almost immediately.

I have some time in the afternoon. Anything urgent?

No. Personal business, not political. Nothing to worry about.

Lunch? Gregory asked.

Prefer it in private, Michaelis said, hoping Gregory wouldn't push and inquire why.

But nothing's wrong? I could do three, but earlier if you need it, Gregory replied.

Nothing's wrong. Three is fine. See you then, he said, and set his phone down again.

CHAPTER NINE

HIS FATHER MIGHT have told him not to worry, but when Michaelis arrived at Gregory's office the following afternoon, something was definitely wrong. He was tense in a very specific way – posture intent, shoulders back, face a careful blank. He wasn't upset or angry; he was confused, and Gregory knew his father well enough to know how much he hated being confused.

"Come over to the window," Gregory said, settling on the bench by his big office window. "I get tired of the desk and you're not a job applicant."

"I thought you were finished with hiring the new staff."

"We are, mostly. Though if you want a job I'm pretty sure there are some open," Gregory said, as Michaelis settled next to him. "It didn't sound serious in text, but it looks pretty serious from here. What's going on?"

"I want to ask you something," Michaelis said. "I think you might have more expertise in some areas than I do. I have a bit of a modern dilemma, but I'm not sure how to ask about it, to be honest." He gave Gregory a dry smile. "Difficult for a man to go to his son for advice."

"If it helps, technically you're also my subject," Gregory said, bumping his shoulder against his father's. "How can the king advise?"

"I don't want to pull you into something that isn't your responsibility," Michaelis said, studying his hands. "And if you don't want to answer any of this, you don't have to."

"Now I'm a little worried," Gregory said. "You're not in some kind of legal trouble, are you?"

"Hah. No. That'd be easier, actually. I know how to pay a bribe."

"Dad!"

"Well, politics was different when I was young." Michaelis slouched backwards, a move Gregory recognized – he did it himself when he was uncertain what to do and annoyed by it. "All right. I know when you came out, lord, a decade ago now, you were older than a lot of people do it these days. You took a while. To be sure of yourself. To know what you wanted to do and how to do it."

"Yeah. You were still the first person I told," Gregory said. "Well. Mom, then you."

"And I'm glad of that. I know I haven't always been perfect about it. I was so pleased you felt you could trust me, and I'm grateful you...tolerated me."

"It wasn't like that," Gregory said quietly. "I could always see you were trying."

"I was," Michaelis agreed. "I was just very worried about how the world would treat you. Never worried about you, yourself."

"I know."

"What I want to know is...how did you know? I know you struggled, you weren't sure...did you just wake up one day knowing, at last?"

Gregory frowned, considering this.

"Well. Around ten or so, you sort of start to get the message that things are going to change, you get told about the birds and bees and that someday you'll find girls interesting for new and exciting reasons," he said at last. "Even in Askazer-Shivadlakia, we're so small, most of the media comes from elsewhere and at least when I was growing up it was very heterosexual. The implication was always that starting to like girls, that's when you start to grow up. It isn't true, but a lot of people think it is."

Michaelis nodded.

"So I kept waiting to grow up, to find girls interesting, and I figured maybe I was just…a late bloomer or something, but I realized eventually that wasn't going to happen. And I wasn't sure what I felt about boys was right, either."

"Oh, no, Gregory – "

"Not like that!" Gregory said hastily. "I didn't think I was *wrong* or something. Maybe I didn't like anyone! I just couldn't be sure what I was feeling. So I had to test it out. And eventually I worked out that it was going to be men, for me. After that I still had to work out how to tell people, or even whether to tell people, given I wanted to be king. I had your public relations office do a poll, did you know?"

"You did what?"

"When I was nineteen. I had them do some secret market research about whether Askazer-Shivadlakia would elect a gay king. Good news is, they came back 91% positive on the idea, and here I am, so well done us."

Michaelis chuckled, which was good – at least he wasn't as panicked as before. "Of course you did market research."

"Got to, these days. The point is, by the time I came out, I had some kind of ground to stand on. But no, it wasn't sudden. It took time."

"And a lot of work, it sounds like."

"Well, I did almost fail French Lit. I was distracted by a boy." Gregory grinned sidelong at him. "Why do you ask? Are you at the chapter in your memoirs where your extremely awkward twenty year old son tells you he's gay? I can come on the podcast and talk about it, if you want. I don't mind."

He could see his father considering how to answer, considering whether to lie. He cut that off quickly.

"Is there something you want to tell me?" he asked. "Like…are you seeing someone? You know it'd be okay. Mom would want you to be happy – "

"That's not exactly it," Michaelis said. "There's a person I care for, yes. I would actually be concerned you wouldn't be comfortable with me seeing someone after your mother passed, so that's good to hear. The problem is that I don't know precisely how I feel, and I don't want to get involved if I'm going to hurt them, even inadvertently. With your mother I knew, in a heartbeat, there was a specific day and hour that I knew, and that knowing didn't go away until she died. I was so certain with her and now nothing in my life is certain, anywhere."

He sounded distressed, like this one thing had somehow managed to put his entire life into a tailspin. Gregory turned on instinct and pulled him into a hug, tugging his father's head down to his shoulder. It said a lot that he went without protest, and stayed there for a while. They weren't really either of them big on hugging, but apparently everything was out the window today.

"It's a lot of change," Gregory said at last. "The last few months. I know how you feel. All this is kind of new to me, too."

Michaelis nodded and finally leaned back. "Thank you."

"Well, however I can continue to be awkward," Gregory said with a smile. Michaelis matched it, then looked away. "Seriously. You know what you and Mom had was not the way these things normally work, right?"

"What?"

"Nobody falls in love with their soulmate in their teens and spends the next few decades happily ruling a country with them. You are literally some kind of fairytale prince," Gregory said. "Most of us have to fight to get something like that. You and Mom were effortless, but that's not how this normally goes."

"You have Edward," Michaelis said.

"I do, yes, and I love him, but he is so much work, you have no idea," Gregory said. "And I dated a lot of people before him, and he dated a lot of people before me. We had breakups and hurt people and got hurt, that's how dating is. What you're feeling now is what the rest of us spent our twenties feeling."

"Oh," Michaelis said.

"Yeah. It's okay to worry about hurting someone if you don't know how you feel, but that's just going to happen sometimes, I'm afraid," Gregory said. "The fact you're worried strongly suggests whoever this person is, you do care about them."

"Mm."

"Dad, listen…is it a guy?" Gregory said. "Because the drift of this conversation reminds me of being twenty again. It's fine if it is, I'm actually on much more solid ground with sexuality crises. There are books I can recommend."

"It's Jes," Michaelis said.

"Ah. Oh. Wow," Gregory said. Immediately, he could see it – Jes was attractive, seemed like an interesting person, and they'd been working together, living in the same building if not the same rooms. It actually explained a few things. "I can see how that would be – "

"Complex, yes," Michaelis agreed. "I do think they're interested, I'm not completely blind to this kind of thing, but the last thing I want to do is begin something and then turn coward. I get the sense Jes has probably had a lot of that in their life. I don't want to add to it."

"Does that seem likely?" Gregory asked hesitantly.

"Not likely, but possible. I don't know, Gregory. I don't know if I could be with anyone who wasn't your mother," Michaelis said, clearly frustrated. "Before now I'd have said I was fine being alone."

"Oh, Dad," Gregory said.

"I was," Michaelis insisted. "And then I met Jes and I had something to occupy my time again. And if it's just that I feel useful around them, them and Noah, that's not enough to sustain anything real."

"You don't know if you like Jes or just the person you are around them," Gregory said. Michaelis nodded. "You really can't do anything by halves in your life, can you?"

"I wouldn't get too smart about it, that gene's in you somewhere too," Michaelis replied.

"Yeah, well, that's Eddie's problem," Gregory replied. "Is this useful at all, what we're doing here?"

"Yes. I think so. It's one more thread to pull on trying to unravel all this," Michaelis said. "I do appreciate it."

"Do you, uh, want the books anyway? There are a couple on genderqueer relationships that might help."

"No. Well. Maybe make sure you know where they are. You know me, I like to muddle through on my own."

"Another thing that will probably eventually become Eddie's problem," Gregory sighed. "What can I do to help?"

"You've done it, as far as you can, I think," his father said. "Just having someone else's perspective is helpful. Do you...like Jes? That matters too, you know."

"From what I've seen of them, yes. But you're a grown man and so am I, I don't have to like the people you date."

"I'd prefer if you did."

"Then yes. I like them," Gregory said. "And I'm pleased you've found something that makes you happy, whether or not you do anything about this potential thing with Jes. Come talk if you need to, you don't have to make an appointment. I'll make time."

"You're the king, you know that's not how this works."

"When I was twelve you canceled Parliament for the day because I was having a nervous breakdown over acne. If you didn't want me to make time for family you shouldn't have led by example," Gregory said with a smile.

"I'm your father, that's different."

"Not really, but that's a discussion we can have some other time. Come talk whenever you need to, I always have time for you. Though maybe not Tuesday nights if you can avoid it."

Michaelis looked at him curiously as they both stood. "What's on Tuesday night that's so vital?"

"Date night with Eddie. It's for your own good, you don't want to walk in on anything."

"Ah. Duly noted." Michaelis hesitated, then hugged Gregory again. "Thank you."

"Anytime," Gregory said. "Even Tuesday if you have to."

When his father was gone, Alanna knocked on the doorway.

"I just saw Michaelis leaving," she said. "He looked confused, and I only know it was confusion because I almost never see that expression on his face."

"He's going through some things," Gregory said vaguely.

"Aren't we all," Alanna replied. "Is he okay?"

"He will be. He usually is. Ready for afternoon debrief?"

"Of course. Excitingly, the first of the building projects should go through budget approval tomorrow…"

It was not a long walk back to the lodge from the palace, and Michaelis felt that he could use a truly long walk right now. He thought better when he was moving, and the lake felt mockingly serene. How dare it be so scenic when human beings had to deal with turmoil like this?

He almost laughed. He was much too old to be so dramatic, even being Shivadh. Still, instead of taking the trail around the lake back to the lodge, he took the road directly down into Fons-Askaz. At least the act of having to keep out of the way of foot traffic and cars felt suitably chaotic.

He was conscious, in a way he wasn't usually, of the murmurs that surrounded and followed him. Locals knew him and didn't care much, but the tourists were thick on the ground and all of them clearly recognized him, some consulting the cash bills in their hands for comparison. He kept his expression abstracted – not forbidding, just a little distant and, hopefully, unapproachable. He saw one person take a selfie with him in the background, but ignored it.

What was the point of having trained to rule, having ruled

for decades, and having graciously handed over rule to his son, if he couldn't get a handle on this? Gregory was right, hurting people was sometimes simply a part of having relationships with them, and that obviously meant this shouldn't happen. Jes didn't deserve that and Noah certainly didn't. Even if he did know how to handle this, the possibility was still there that he'd screw it up. So, he would need to figure out a way around it.

That, at least, was a plan. It let him slow his pace a little, his shoulders relaxing a fraction. Fine; that was a problem to solve instead of an intractable roadblock.

He turned down an alley off the high street, stopping at the little side-door bakery he knew was there. They had a nice new awning with a more prominent sign, probably on account of the increased tourism, and also a few new items in the bakery case. One of them was a pastry that looked like a panda – the sign in front of it read "PAIN-DA CHOCOLAT" – and Michaelis examined it with curiosity.

"You would not believe how many tourists buy them just to take a photo," the baker said with a grin. "You make one cute pain au chocolat or a clever sort of cake, you've made your sales for the week."

"Why a panda, though?" Michaelis asked.

"Who knows, Your Grace? My daughter suggested it. Someone else was already doing birds and rabbits."

"Hm. Well, it's still your pain au chocolat, isn't it? Two of the pandas in a box, and a sausage roll – the lamb, if you have it."

"Want the roll hot?"

"Please."

Bakery box dangling from his fingers and sausage roll in hand, he felt a little better about the world. There was a scenic overlook on the harbor not far away; while the promenade had a number of people on it, the benches were empty. He sat and ate and watched people come and go, letting things simmer until he felt ready to consider them. That was the way his mind worked, he knew that well enough – it took time for the gears to grind all the way around, but he could be patient.

His phone beeped, eventually, and he looked down to a text from Eddie.

Don't jump :D it read, and he opened it to find a screengrab of a Photogram of himself. Someone had taken his picture, sitting on the bench, looking contemplative, and posted it while he was still sitting there.

They'd captioned the photo *Nice to know even the former king has sadness dinner sometimes.*

He considered it, then texted back, *Edward, life has become very recursive.*

Not sure what that means, but let me know if you need a ride home or someone to talk to, Eddie replied.

No, I'm fine. It wasn't a sadness dinner, it was a nice snack.

Eddie sent him a thumbs-up icon. Michaelis sat back and let a smile drift across his face, just in case anyone else was concerned. A few people nodded to him as they passed and he nodded back. Eventually he stretched a little, rising to go to the railing and watch a sailboat tacking into the harbor.

One thing he had learned in his career was the control of strong emotions. Especially when he was new on the throne, he couldn't show if he was upset or angry about something. He'd thought of himself not as two people but as two parts of a person – the king, and Michaelis. Back then, if Michaelis was angry, he slipped into being the king. A little distant, very dignified, full of authority. He'd been twenty-one when he was crowned. What else could he do?

He hadn't had to use that kind of thinking in years. As one got older, all the politics seemed increasingly petty. Important, but not important enough for passion. He'd developed a level head, and he just needed to find the level again.

Well, he'd done it once; he could simply retreat a little into the king again, when things got intense. It would protect both him and Jes, and nobody would come to harm. If they couldn't have that...potential, as Gregory called it, well, one couldn't have everything in this life.

Content with this, he turned from the sailboat, docking safely in harbor, and began the walk back to the lodge.

When he let himself in, Noah and Jes were in the kitchen; Jes looked up from their half-eaten dinner and smiled. Michaelis nodded and held up the bakery box.

"Wait until you see what nonsense I found," he said, and Noah took the box from him while Jes kicked out a chair so he could sit.

"PANDA CROISSANTS," Noah crowed. Jes took the one he handed them and tore into it with delight while Noah looked for the best lighting to photograph his.

And the king Michaelis had decided to be, his very important and careful armor, simply evaporated. All his resolve and his plans, gone in a flash. He couldn't even regret it.

There was a restaurant in town – near the bakery, actually – that had nice views of the water and did extremely good pasta. He was pretty sure he could get a reservation there without too much trouble. He'd wait a few days, make sure the weather would be fine, and ask Jes to have dinner with him, as a date, to see how it would go.

It would have worked, probably.

Instead, it was all Noah's fault.

Michaelis had found the restaurant's phone number, and had meant to speak to the palace scheduler, who could swing him both the best table and an ideal time, but his days were so busy now. He was recording a new episode with Noah most of the morning, and in the afternoon he had retakes to do with Jes, as well as some kind of weird sound check Lachlan was insisting on.

They were nearly done, at least he hoped, and Lachlan was talking about possible vocal rest and not having any dairy for a week, when Jes's phone went berserk.

Michaelis, blinking at the strobe lights and sirens coming from the phone, jerked backwards. Jes grabbed the phone and fumbled to silence it, while Lachlan leapt up from his seat.

"What the hell was that?" Michaelis asked, but Jes just held up a finger and set the phone down, tapping the answer-call button on the screen.

"Noah, is that you?" they asked.

"Emergency ringtone," Lachlan said to Michaelis softly. "Noah uses it if he needs to interrupt recording."

"Hey Boss," Noah said, voice staticky over the speakerphone. "Can you hear me okay?"

"Sure can. What's going on? You're echoing – where are you?"

"Uh, you remember when Michaelis said there was a secret wine cellar?" Noah asked.

"No – did you tell him that?" Jes asked, looking at Michaelis.

"I'm here, Noah. I do remember saying that," Michaelis said. "It was just a rumor, though."

"I think I found it," Noah said. "I kinda fell in. You might have to come get me out."

"Wild Child, I am going to tie you to a chair," Jes said. "Are you okay?"

"Nothing bleeding," Noah said cheerfully.

"That's not an answer," Michaelis said. From the look on Jes's face he wasn't the only one startled by how stern he sounded.

"Might have a twisted ankle. Nothing else hurts," Noah said, more meekly. "It is dark and the spiders are large, so if you could hurry…"

"Where are you, relative to the recording booths?" Jes asked, getting up with the phone and walking out into the bunker. Michaelis followed, Lachlan on his heels.

"Okay, so the room Michaelis said was the bunker's nursery?" Noah said.

"Yes, I know the one," Michaelis answered, leading them across the big meeting space and through the doorway.

"There's a hallway on the other side," Noah said.

"The one that goes to the north end of the garage?"

"Yeah, that one. You know the weird wood panel in the middle of the wall?"

"Yes, my son," Jes said, voice turning vaguely threatening, and Michaelis could see why – the panel had been pulled down and laid on the floor. "Noah, did you – how did you even get that off the wall?"

"I didn't! It fell off, I heard it fall so I came to investigate," Noah said over the speaker. They could hear his actual voice as well, if only faintly. "There's a secret room behind it! You try to resist a secret room!"

"I'm gonna hang up, we can hear you," Jes said, and put the phone away. "Noah!"

"I think there is actually a lot of wine here!" Noah's voice drifted in.

Jes climbed through the strange, half-plastered hole the wooden panel had been covering. Michaelis eyed it warily.

"This is some nonsense haunted-house bullshit," Lachlan yelled through the gap.

"Thanks, Uncle Lachlan, I want that on a t-shirt," Noah called back.

"Michaelis! Lachlan! Stop being dipshits and come in here!" Jes yelled. Michaelis let Lachlan squeeze through and then followed, scraping up his face when he met an unexpected jut of broken wood in the wall.

"Girl, the demolition of it all," Lachlan said, joining Jes at the edge of a gaping hole in the floor of the weird little room they were in. Unlike the rest of the bunker, it had dirt walls and wood floors.

"It's a miracle he even got a phone signal out to you," Michaelis said, using the light from his phone to study the wooden beams propping up ceiling panels, which were showing distinct signs of rot – warping and flaking, eaten away completely in places, and cracked badly in others.

"The wifi can get in here from the hallway," Noah called up. "I wouldn't go anywhere in the lodge that I couldn't get wifi."

"Nice to know you have one boundary," Michaelis drawled.

"Did you fall through?" Jes asked. "You sound like you're about twenty feet down."

"Only a little," Noah said. "The hole was already here. There used to be stairs at one end. I kinda fell through the last few stairs and then they fell in after me."

"He's very calm about this," Michaelis said to Lachlan.

"He's the only one," Lachlan replied. Jes lit up the flashlight on their phone and aimed it down the hole, catching Noah's dirty but apparently unharmed face.

"I don't think even Lachlan's going to be able to reach you," they said.

"I am not dangling my ass down into that hole unless I have to, either," Lachlan replied.

"Can we call the fire department? Or, um, a mountaineer?" Noah suggested.

"I don't want you in that hole a second longer than necessary. This entire room isn't stable," Michaelis said.

"Well, unless you can levitate me out…"

"Rope," Michaelis said. Jes looked up at him. "There's plenty upstairs. Stay here with him and try not to move around too much. I'll get some rope and a pulley."

"What the fuck do we do with a pulley?" he heard Lachlan ask, but he was already slipping back out into the hallway, running full-tilt for the stairs.

Upstairs he headed for the supply shed next to the lodge. It was a catch-all for anything one might need – spare oars and swimsuits, fishing poles and bows, camping gear, and emergency supplies. No ladders, which was something he was going to address at a future date. He pulled down two coils of rope that looked relatively new, then rummaged for a pulley, which fortunately came already attached to a tripod – he guessed it was for getting small boats in and out of the water. After a second of consideration, he also took a knife from the shelf and a plastic tarp from the pile near the door.

He had to shove it all through the gap before he could get through, Lachlan taking the supplies while Jes kept up a running conversation with Noah.

"He's recording it, because of course he is," Lachlan said.

"Great content, though," Michaelis replied, even as he became aware it was probably not the appropriate thing to say.

"I know, I'm so pissed he thought of it first," Lachlan replied.

"Okay, Noah, I'm going to drop a tarp and a knife down to you," Michaelis said, kneeling at the edge. The only light in the room was Jes's phone light, lying on the floor next to them; he should have thought to take a lantern as well. "While we get this set up, you cut the tarp into strips. I want you to wrap your arms in them from palm to elbow, because that's where you're going to lock the rope, around your arms. The tarp will protect your skin. How are you at a dead hang?"

"What the hell's a dead hang?" Noah asked, sounding alarmed.

"Never mind. Just get to work," Michaelis said, and let the tarp fall. "Knife coming down, watch yourself," he added, and leaned as far into the hole as he could before dropping it. The floorboards creaked ominously.

"If the floor gives way I am going to throw a shit fit that will be so loud it'll get us rescued," Lachlan said.

"Don't brag if you can't back it up," Michaelis advised, examining the tripod. The problem was the size of the hole and relative smallness of the room – no space for the tripod to actually sit. They'd have to just use it as a pole. "Here. We can't sit this on the floor so someone's going to have to hold it here at an angle. Do you think you can keep this steady while I pull Noah up with it?" he asked, handing the pole to Jes so they could test the weight.

"Lachlan, come help," Jes said, fixing their arms around the pole and leaning back. Lachlan got in front of them, resting it across his shoulders.

"I'll hold, you anchor," he said, and Jes moved back to keep the tip of it steady on the floor.

Michaelis unwound one of the coils of rope and began feeding it through the pulley, the same as he'd hitch it to bring a boat out onto a dock.

"Start getting ready to brace now," he said, as he paid out the rope, hanging over the open gap. "Noah, let me know when it touches ground."

"Got it!" Noah said.

"Great. Grab it at shoulder height and wrap your arms in it, so that it locks in place."

"Like the guys who do the silk acrobatics," Noah said.

"Sure," Michaelis agreed. "Let me know when you're ready. I'm going to pull you up but if you can keep your abdomen tense and your knees lifted we'll get you up a little faster. Safer, too."

"I'm ready!"

"This is going to be really ugly for about three minutes," Michaelis said, and began to pull.

Lachlan groaned and then swore, not especially obscenely but still quite imaginatively. Jes grunted and kicked one foot out to brace themself, heel digging into the soft wood. Michaelis pulled hand over hand, as fast as he dared, throwing his weight back on each tug, gradually moving backwards. Noah's arms appeared above the gap and then his face; when his shoes were visible, Lachlan swung the pole sharply to the left.

Noah and Lachlan tumbled onto the wood floor together and the pole clattered to the ground; Jes skidded in the opposite direction, and Michaelis went backwards with a thump, now that the tension was off the ropes. He gasped for a second, breath knocked out of him, and then pushed himself up on his elbows.

Lachlan was helping Noah to his feet and hustling him towards the door; Jes was scrambling up to offer Michaelis a hand, and he let himself be tugged to a sitting position, then got his first deep breath and pushed himself upright as Jes gathered up their phone.

"Go, this isn't safe," he said. "I'll follow, just get up to the lodge."

They nodded and slipped out, and he cut himself again getting through, but at least nothing collapsed before he managed it. It took him a while to climb the stairs, still winded, but the chaos upstairs was at least under control when he arrived.

Noah was sitting on the kitchen counter, getting checked over by Jes. Lachlan fussed around the boy, helping him get the crumpled tarp off his arms and clucking over the bruising there. Jes, satisfied there were no broken bones, noticed Lachlan's skinned elbows, and got the first aid kit from under the sink. Michaelis, still getting his lung capacity back, leaned in the doorway and watched, gently stretching his arms.

He was just starting to think about quietly disappearing to clean the dust and sweat off himself when Lachlan turned around and blurted "CARRIE!" at him in a panicked voice.

"Oh, shit, Michaelis," Jes said, fumbling the first aid kit. He looked behind him, wondering what was wrong.

"Your face," Lachlan said, as Jes set the kit on the counter and went to him, pulling him into the kitchen. They held up his hand in theirs, staring at it. He realized his knuckles and palms were scraped raw, red rivulets drying in tracks down his wrists on both arms. To his shock, his shirt was covered in still-damp blood.

"It looks worse than it is," he said, confused. "Nothing hurts, they can't be that deep. I don't know where all the rest of the blood is from – "

"Inside you!" Lachlan yelped.

Jes was wetting a towel in the sink, and he saw their hands shaking from the adrenaline crash as they carried it over. They rubbed the cool towel gently against his forehead, bringing it away stained red, and then ran it down one cheek –

His face erupted in sudden, stinging pain, like antiseptic ointment on road rash. He let out a startled bellow.

"Found where the blood came from," Jes said. "Sorry, I'll be gentler."

He braced for a second swipe and managed to hold still, even when Lachlan actually did follow Jes's cleaning with spray antiseptic. The pain in his face, at least, kept his mind off the newly discovered rope burn on his palms that Jes was trying to clean. He heard Noah taking pictures behind them and shot the boy a scolding glare.

"You really tore yourself up," Lachlan said. "If there is any good wine down there, you should call dibs."

"I think it's probably state property," Michaelis said.

"Not if the state never finds out about it. If you don't want it, at least let me loose before you report it. Ah, scalp wound," Lachlan added, working his way around behind Michaelis's ear. "Lie back and think of Askaz, darling."

Lachlan finally got everything disinfected to his high standards, and Jes wrapped the worst of the rope burns in gauze. When they were finished, Noah got off the counter, eyes huge and sad in the way only drama-filled adolescence allowed.

"I'm really sorry," he said. "I didn't want anyone to get hurt."

"We know, Wild Child," Lachlan said quietly.

"You've got to be careful," Jes said, sounding more anxious than angry. They rubbed his back. "We'll talk about it later. You're not in any trouble and I'm sure seeing what happened to Michaelis is punishment enough if you were."

"Sorry, Michaelis," Noah practically whispered, head hanging low.

Michaelis rested a bandaged hand on Noah's arm, wincing, and then pulled him forward. As soon as he was close enough, he wrapped him in a hug, face pressed to his dusty hair.

"Small price to pay to get you out safely," he said, as Noah's arms wrapped around his waist. "Glad you weren't hurt, Tavat."

Jes, he could see, recognized the word, though Lachlan and Noah clearly didn't. He let go and held Noah away from him, giving him a quick once-over.

"Why don't you go wash up? If anything starts to hurt, call Jes at once," he ordered, and gave Noah a gentle push.

"I'm gonna make sure everything in the studio gets saved and shut down properly," Lachlan said, moving towards the bunker stairs. "Nobody fall through anything until I get back, I have an extremely delicate constitution for this kind of thing."

Michaelis took the towel from Jes, refolding it to find a clean patch. He pulled his bloody shirt off and tried to rub his neck clean. Jes turned and sat on the counter, next to him. After a minute or two, they laughed and put their hands on their head.

"That was really, really scary," they said. "My child almost literally fell down a well like in an old Lassie movie."

"He's definitely your kid," Michaelis said, moving to stand in front of them, still trying to get blood and grime off his neck. "But also, I'm pretty sure having an unstable secret wine cellar hidden behind a warped old board in the hallway is a liability."

"Are you saying I should sue?"

"Rather hoping you won't, but you'd have grounds," he said. They leaned forward and rested their forehead on his bare shoulder. He covered the nape of their neck with one hand and leaned his head to the side, speaking quietly, mouth close to their ear. "He's safe, Jes. Kids get into scrapes. Of all the dangerous stuff he could do at his age, this is remarkably wholesome."

"I'm still terrified."

"What kind of parent would you be if you weren't? He's not even my kin and I was scared, too."

"Bet King Gregory never fell in a wine hole."

"My son once crashed a golf cart into a water hazard and nearly drowned half the royal cousins and himself."

"That doesn't sound like him. Was he drinking?"

"No, he was seven. But he definitely did the driving on purpose, which is more than you can accuse Noah of. Did get me out of ever having to go golfing again, which I hated, so in the end I suppose I should be grateful."

Jes rested their fingertips against his ribs, trembling slowly subsiding. They turned their head further, pressing their nose into the hollow of his throat.

"Jes – " he began, worried.

"Please, don't make me feel weird about this," Jes said. "I just – "

"No, no, shh," he said. "I'm not objecting."

He considered his next words carefully. Jes, apparently not aware they were supposed to wait, lifted their head and kissed him.

He felt like he sort of tumbled into it, letting them run the show, until good sense kicked in and he pulled away gently. He didn't go far; no one had that much self-control.

"Can't get a word in edgewise with you," he said. Jes laughed nervously. They looked a mess. He slid his hand around from where it still cupped the back of their head, so that he could cradle their cheek.

"I want this very badly," he said in a low voice. "I've seen enough to know you probably do too. But there's some reason you always pull back, and I've never pushed it either. That's fine, I didn't expect it to go anywhere. This, now, is a stress reaction, and that's fine too. It just means...I'm not going to hold you to anything you do right now, and I'm not going to do much until I know you're really good with this. Or until we're both more in our right minds. Now is not a good time for this. Later will work just as well."

"I was worried it might endanger the network, us getting

entangled. We were working in your home, and then we moved into it…and I was worried about Noah," they said. "If it went badly. He might get caught in the crossfire. I never, ever wanted him to get trapped between two people who hate each other."

"Not like your parents," he guessed. They nodded miserably. "I would never hurt that boy intentionally. Or you."

"Yeah, I'm seeing that," they said.

Michaelis leaned in slowly, giving Jes time to meet him halfway. When they kissed, he could taste chalky plaster dust and his own blood. Jes pushed forward and his mouth opened, scrapes on his cheek singing in pain. It felt spectacular, dangerous and satisfying. He stepped in and slid his free hand around their waist, their arms resting on his shoulders. When he finally retreated, because he could hear footsteps, they looked dazed.

"Lachlan's on the stairs," he said. "We'll talk later? Perhaps tonight?"

Jes nodded and gave him a quick last kiss, then turned in time to see Lachlan emerge from below.

"You both look like you've been through a small war," he said. "Not to be the pragma queen instead of the drama queen but Jes, we are going to need to rebook the last few appointments for studio time today, unless you want me to keep going."

"No, that's not fair to you or them. I can help call and make the changes," they said, glancing at Michaelis.

"I should make some calls about the wine cellar. We're going to need a structural engineer and a historian, which sounds like the start of a joke," Michaelis said. "I'll do it from my rooms."

He showered first and then called Gregory, who was equal parts alarmed and intrigued. They had to have a brief debate about whether Michaelis or Noah needed formal medical care, which required a promise to see a doctor if anything else started to hurt, but eventually Gregory agreed that rest was probably best. He forwarded the call to the palace switchboard, which connected Michaelis to the head of the historical society. By the time he'd made all the necessary explanations and arrangements with three separate offices of the palace, he was exhausted and crashing fast. He dropped onto the bed to rest for a few minutes, and more or less passed out.

He woke when someone sat on the edge of the bed; Jes, it turned out, looking clean but weary. He sat up, leaning in from behind, and didn't so much kiss their shoulder as tiredly rest his mouth there. They raised a hand to stroke his hair, cautious of the long cut on his scalp.

"How's Noah?" he asked.

"Lachlan's watching a movie with him. I said I'd see how you were doing."

"No worse than I was..." He looked at his watch, "...an hour ago when I was having a very surreal conversation with the royal sommelier. And how are you?"

"Better. I know now's probably not what you meant when you said later, but I have questions."

"It's all right. I've had some rest and you've had a bath, so we could be worse," he said. Jes didn't laugh.

"You said you want this," they said.

He propped his chin on their shoulder. "Indeed."

"I don't get the sense that you're casual about dating."

"You are very correct."

"And I don't do that unless I think someone is going to be around for a while, for me but also for Noah. People who are safe. Stable."

"I'm doing my best," he said.

They turned to give him a quick kiss. "I know. Which puts a lot of my worries to rest. But I also need to know that if we do this, you're going to be cool with my identity – and yours. That you aren't going to bolt because you're too straight for this."

"I was worried about that too. I didn't want to give you a false impression. Asked Gregory for some advice, actually," he said. "It helped, but I couldn't really talk to him about some things. Not a child's job to help his father out like that."

"How do you mean? Incidentally, I'd love to hear Eddie's take on this."

"I considered it, but I didn't feel ready for what I might hear from the sage Eddie Rambler. What I couldn't tell Gregory was that – I loved his mother, but it was for her, the…essence of who she was. If she'd been a man I might still have loved her, I don't know. And Gregory reminded me that what we had was unusual; we spoke this weird personal language for each other."

"So…*are* you straight?" Jes asked, looking perplexed and concerned.

"I'm not often attracted to anyone, to be honest. I think perhaps because there was no room for that while Miranda was alive, and we fell in love when I was eighteen. After she passed, well, grief tends to smother that kind of thing. In my limited experience, all of the people I've felt attraction to have been women until now, but I don't have a problem with the fact that you aren't one. I like you, Jes, and I want you. There are reasons this might not work, but…I was planning to ask you to dinner before all this happened."

He kissed their throat, then leaned forward as they twisted around to kiss him on the mouth.

"Well, maybe you are a little queer, then," they said, amused. He held up his thumb and forefinger, slightly apart, and they nodded. "When were you making moves, anyway? You said you never pushed. When did you even drop hints?"

"Jes," Michaelis said. "Did you think I was walking around shirtless after swimming because I wanted to air dry?"

"Oh. Well. That was very nice," they said. "I said hello to your biceps every morning."

"Glad to hear it." He leaned close, voice soft. "I enjoyed it. I had no expectations, but I saw you noticing. I liked that."

Jes turned to him, impulsively. "Let me take you to dinner tomorrow instead," they said. "Instead of you taking me, I mean."

"Sounds fine," he said. "But I'm willing to put out now. How much time do you think we have?"

"They're watching *Dune*."

"So we could do dinner and at least half an hour of foreplay and still have plenty of time."

"How much foreplay did you intend?" Jes asked, sounding intrigued.

"Dealer's choice," he replied. They kissed him again, deep but gentle.

"You're right, this is coming from stress," they said. "No need to rush."

He nodded but didn't move away; they both sat there for a while, touching quietly, until he sighed.

"What?" they asked.

"I'm going to have to wear concealer to make the scrapes on my face look less intense," he said. "First time I've ever been the one putting on makeup for a date."

They smiled, patting his cheek. "If you want, I know a lipstick that would look killer on you."

"Pass, but I appreciate the thought. Next time I have to wear some for television, maybe."

"Get some more sleep. One of us will wake you for dinner," they said. "I'm going to go listen to Lachlan rhapsodize about Sting's abs."

"Oh, it's the David Lynch one? We could have a whole relationship before that one finishes. Have fun," Michaelis replied, as Jes stood and headed for the door. They turned and gave him a smile so bright and full of promise that he didn't manage to speak before they'd gone.

He slept a little more, waking eventually when his scrapes started to bother him. He found a clean shirt and walked, slow and stiff, out to the front of the lodge. Jes and Noah were both asleep on the couch, *Dune* still going on mute, and Lachlan was in the kitchen.

"Sit, I'll bring you something," Lachlan said. "It's only canned soup, but it's hot and salty, just like me."

Michaelis nodded gratefully, seating himself and taking the bowl with care.

"How are your scrapes?" Lachlan asked.

"Not too bad. Bet you're bruised to hell from holding up that pulley," Michaelis said.

"Back's going to be purple all over," Lachlan said good naturedly. "But like you told Noah, it's a small price to pay."

Michaelis nodded. Lachlan studied him.

"You said something else, too, when you said that. Something you called Noah," he said. "Tavan?"

"Tavat."

"Is that like a new name he's trying out, or a nickname or something? Unless you're not allowed to tell me."

Michaelis shook his head. "I just said it in the moment. It's in the old Shivadh language. You're not Shivadh by birth."

"No, I'm from Massachusetts. Married in. Jes introduced us, actually. Why?"

"It's a little complicated. We have this…legal tradition, not a law but more of a cultural rule, that some things only princes are allowed to do. But because we are exactly that arrogant, we also say, well, every Shivadh is royalty, everyone is a prince, so anyone can do these forbidden royal things if they dare to. Tavat is what you call a person who is so self-assured that they, as an ordinary person, act like a royal."

"So it's a compliment. Like calling someone brash or daring. Oh! Like the Shivadh version of Wild Child, right?"

Michaelis gave him a measuring look, but Lachlan, as loud as he could be, wasn't indiscreet.

"Yes, coming from anyone else," he admitted. "Coming from me, it's different. Usually you'd translate it to English, especially for a youngster like Noah, as something like…princeling. Little daring prince. But I'm the king. Former king. So when I call someone Tavat, it's layered."

"Almost like saying he's an adopted son," Lachlan said quietly.

"I care about both of them."

Lachlan nodded. "My husband and I adopted. She was only a few days old."

"I listened to the podcast about it. Sounds harrowing."

"It was, but I wouldn't trade it. I would absolutely jump in a wine hole to keep my child from getting a bumped head, let alone anything worse."

"Then she's a very lucky child." Michaelis smiled. "But even if I didn't feel...paternal towards Noah, he is Tavat anyway, you know. A Shivadh princeling if ever I met one. If he manages to survive to adulthood I'll be interested to see where life takes him."

Lachlan sipped his drink. "And Jes?"

Michaelis looked past him to where Jes was sleeping, Noah tucked up against them.

"I didn't know them when they were young, but yes, I'm sure they would have been considered Tavat. Leaving home so young, returning in triumph years later, that's practically mythological. If I were still king, I'd need to coin a word for them. Caez, I think."

"What does Caez mean?"

"Some words for king, like Kaiser and Tsar – and, incidentally, Askaz – descend from the Latin, Caesar. It's a family name, but obviously when we think of Caesar we think of emperors, of men. Caez is just a...part of a word. There's no gender involved. It would be a neutral name for a monarch, or the spouse of one."

"Do you mean you'd call them that, or you'd make them one?" Lachlan asked, arching a brow.

Michaelis arched one back. "Objections either way?"

"Only that you two come from pretty different worlds. But Jes is old enough to look after themselves. You looked after a country, I assume you can handle them." Lachlan glanced over his shoulder. "It was hard for them to come back here. You made that easier, so I'm inclined to be grateful. And you're pretty, so it's hard to hold much against you," he added with a grin.

"Been skating on my looks all my life, no reason to stop now," Michaelis said, taking a sip of the broth left in his bowl. "Stay here if you want, but I suspect you'd like to go home and have your husband fuss over those bruises. I can look after Jes and Noah."

Lachlan nodded. "Thanks. I'll see you tomorrow, probably?"

"Sure. Unless Noah's not feeling up to recording."

"Are you sure you will be?"

"It's all surface," Michaelis said, gesturing at his face. Lachlan looked skeptical. "Well, we'll know tomorrow."

Lachlan nodded and gathered his keys and briefcase, leaving quietly enough that neither Deimos woke. Michaelis tidied what he could in the kitchen, then went into the living room and gently settled on the sofa next to Noah, resting an arm over his shoulders, palm on Jes's bicep on Noah's other side. Noah woke and turned to look up at him, curious.

"Go back to sleep, unless you want some dinner," Michaelis said softly. "Lachlan went home, but I'll be here."

Noah nodded and closed his eyes again, head tilting over to rest against Michaelis's shoulder. Michaelis tugged the remote gently out of Jes's hand and flicked the channel over from *Dune* to the news, but he spent more time watching light play over Jes's face than he did watching the muted television.

CHAPTER TEN

A TRIO OF people arrived at the lodge the following morning, and looked horrified when Michaelis answered the door.

"Your Grace," Joann, the historian from the palace, gaped at him. "What happened?"

"Lost a fight with the wine cellar," Michaelis replied with a smile, gesturing them inside. Overnight, bright blue-purple bruises had developed around the scrapes, which themselves were angry and red. "Please, come in."

"Did you actually go exploring in it?" a rough-hewn man asked. "I'm Bennet, by the way, Your Grace. I'm the engineer."

"Pleasure," Michaelis replied. "No, one of my guests fell in, and we had a time getting him out. It's why I wanted you out here today, to make sure nothing further collapses."

Hugo, the palace sommelier, gave him a nod. He'd come to Askazer-Shivadlakia with his brother Simon when they'd been hired for the kitchen, and Michaelis had known him a long time; he was interested to see how he'd react to what might be down there.

"There should be coffee, if you'd like some," he said, leading them down the stairs. "And Noah – the boy who fell in – says he's okay to answer some questions about what he saw."

"Oh, the one you're working with!" Joann said. "I've been listening to your podcast – both of them, actually. A bit fast and loose with some of the history but one can't expect rigorous scholarship for something like that."

"Well, I'm happy to get notes," Michaelis said. "But right now, the cellar's my concern."

Jes and Noah were in the kitchen downstairs, going over something on a tablet; Noah waved when he saw them, and Jes shot Michaelis a warm smile. He gave them a nod.

"So – coffee, or would you like to speak with Noah here, if he's free, or do you want to see the cellar first?" he asked.

"Boss canceled all my stuff today," Noah said. "I can show them if you want, Michaelis."

"I'd like to see it, and to speak with you, Noah," Joann said. "Hugo's interested in whether you took notes on any of the vintages."

"Yeah, I got some pictures," Noah said. "Okay, come on."

"Do not go in that room again," Jes cautioned. "And don't eyeroll me!" they added, as Noah gave them a tolerant look. He led the trio off, already talking with Joann, and Michaelis accepted a cup of coffee from Jes gratefully.

"He seems to have bounced back," he said.

"Faster than I will," Jes agreed. "Or you. Those scrapes look nasty this morning."

"I was thinking about that," Michaelis said. "I really would like to have a few days to heal up before I'm out in public and subject to Photogram. I don't want to postpone," he added, before Jes could say anything, "just perhaps to do something a little more private. I thought about asking Simon if he'd do a nice meal for the two of us, but I didn't want to presume."

Jes grinned into their coffee. "Good, I like dancing lead in this relationship."

"I thought you might. Hence asking," he said.

"Hm. Let me think about it. I'm sure I can cook something up that will keep your poor scratched-up face out of the limelight," they said. "I did cancel the recording with Noah today, so you're free to fly off if you like."

"No, I'll stay close. Just in case."

"I know how you feel," Jes said. "Very sweet with that nickname, by the way. Tavat."

"I thought you recognized it. Lachlan asked me to explain it. I think he's clocked us."

"He won't say anything to anyone. Noah hasn't asked about it? Tavat, I mean."

"He probably doesn't remember. I'll talk to him about it eventually. I know there's not much to this whole idea of genetic personality, but he is so Shivadh, Jes. Tavat to his bones."

"I know. I was hoping he'd be a little milder than I was. I guess he hasn't run away from home yet and he doesn't seem to hate me, so progress is steady but slow."

"Well, at least he's somewhere people understand. And if I'm not recording today I'll just keep an eye on the cellar project, maybe run up to the palace to let Gregory know what's going on." He bent to kiss them, the movement surprisingly natural. "Don't work too hard today."

In the hallway, Bennet the engineer was carefully widening the hole in the wall with a crowbar and a mallet, squaring off corners and breaking away the rough ends of wood that had scraped Michaelis as he'd gone in and out. He had a slim lantern with blinding LEDs set up just inside the entry.

"This used to be a door before it was a hole," he said, as Michaelis approached. "I don't know when or how this happened, but you were right to get everyone out of here as fast as possible. The soil's been eating the wood for decades."

"That wood panel's been there since I can remember – at least forty years," Michaelis said.

"Wouldn't surprise me." Bennet poked his head through. "It's a mess in here. I can't let you folks in until I get scaffolding up."

"How long?" Hugo inquired.

"To scaffold the interior? Couple of hours. I'm going to have to build out a walkway to the hole in there, get down, brace the floor from underneath, then put more bracing in up here. I can put in some kind of dumbwaiter thing so you can get the wine out.

I'll have to haul out debris anyway. You two oughta take the kid and go talk to him somewhere more comfortable, this won't be ready for anyone until well after lunch."

Michaelis gave Noah a look, silently asking if he wanted company; Noah shook his head and led Hugo and Joann back the way they'd come.

"Guess this is what nailed you," Bennet said, hefting a chunk of wood.

"I didn't even feel it at the time," Michaelis said. "By the time we got Noah out, I looked like an extra from a horror film."

"Honestly? You're lucky you didn't bring the entire floor down when you pulled him up," Bennet said.

"Should we have waited?" he asked.

"No, that'd just increase the risk, and it's probably cold down there. Looks like a natural cavern of some kind from the photos, and those don't warm up in summer. He'd have risked frostbite or hypothermia if he was down too long. He said you rigged a pulley – good thinking."

Michaelis smiled. "Thank you. Not a skill I've often had to put to use."

"So this is the famous lost wine cellar," Bennet said. "Suppose you want lots of documentation. Photos and such."

"As much as you can. I'm more concerned about any kind of collapse affecting the rest of the building. Is the lodge safe to use?"

"Oh yeah. This is outside the footprint of the rest of the building. I'll get upstairs and mark off outside where it is so you don't walk there – that's a sinkhole waiting to happen – but the bunker's sound, and the lodge is anchored to the bunker. Safe as can be."

"It was absolutely terrifying," Michaelis said, unsure why he was confessing this to the man whose main responsibility in the palace was making sure nothing fell down. "I was very worried for Noah. Jes was in here and they'd fall if the floor collapsed...I wasn't sure we could get him out with just the rope, either."

"I can imagine," Bennet said sympathetically. "I've been in one or two collapses – after the fact, of course, to brace them up. I was in that one you got a bug in the king's ear about, the office building by the harbor?"

"Yes. I saw the roof fall in on that one."

"Well, either you're cursed to cause building collapses, or blessed to survive them," the man said.

"I suspect it's not me," Michaelis said. "Noah's got a knack for trouble."

"So it's for the best you're around. Go on, I'll take it from here. I know where the loading dock is. Better call some of my people to help out. You mind us doing the work today?"

"Better today than later."

Bennet tipped an imaginary hat. "Then good morning to you, Your Grace. Next time you see me you'll be standing in a safe wine cellar, hopefully sampling some of the good stuff."

"If there's anything salvageable I'll see you get a bottle," Michaelis said, and went to make sure Hugo wasn't being excessively French at Noah.

"I have a thought," Jes said to him, when he returned to the kitchen.

"I've heard your work, you have many thoughts," he replied.

"About the date," they said. "But it's a little different from what you or I were thinking of."

"Well, I'm open to ideas."

"Lachlan's mother-in-law, Carla, made a standing invitation to us to come for Friday dinner," they said. "Tomorrow's Friday, you could come with us. It'd get us out of the lodge and be sort of like a date. But low-key because there'll be like five other people on the date. Including Lachlan's baby daughter and my teenage son."

Michaelis let a smile spread across his face. "Jes, that sounds delightful."

"Are you sure?" Jes asked. It was obvious they hadn't thought he'd like the idea.

"We didn't meet in a vacuum," he said. "Noah's important to both of us. Lachlan's good opinion is important to me, too, and I've wanted to meet his husband. A family dinner sounds about our speed, don't you think?"

"Well, we can ditch everyone else afterward if we want to. Dinner's usually over by about eight and Carla likes to kick us out by nine."

"Are you coming to dinner, Michaelis?" Noah asked, arriving with Hugo still in tow.

"Yes, I think so," Michaelis said.

"Boss, Great-Aunt Carla said there's an art fair in town on Saturday so I can sleep over if I want and you say it's fine," Noah said.

Michaelis gestured at Jes, trying to indicate *even better.*

"All right, but you have to text me goodnight and send photos from the fair," Jes said.

"I'm going to take Hugo to see what you've got in the kitchen upstairs. He says he wants to make sure you're restocked," Noah said.

"Don't let him touch the Davzda," Jes said sternly. "I'm saving that."

Friday afternoon, Jes emerged from one of the recording booths to find every surface in the bunker's elderly kitchen covered in dusty bottles of wine.

"I see the cellar's getting cleaned out," they said, studying the bottles on the island curiously. "Anything drinkable?"

"Almost all!" Hugo said excitedly.

"Hugo's over the moon," Michaelis said. "They're doing inventory now. He's helping select some bottles to set aside here at the lodge. Also, I regret this in advance, but…" he nudged a crate with his foot. "That one's full of Davzda."

"Good, we can sell it and put Noah through college," Jes said.

"Actually, some of this does belong to Noah," Michaelis said.

"How do you figure that?"

"Salvage law. He's entitled to ten percent as a finder's fee. By value, not mass, but still. Either you can sell a lot of wine and subsidize his school tuition, or buy him a very nice car, or you'll have great vintages for every life milestone he celebrates. I recommend this one for a wedding," Michaelis added, indicating a cobweb-covered bottle.

"No, surely for a first child," Hugo said. "The red – "

"Hugo, you and red wines," Michaelis sighed.

"Just because you don't like a strong tannin!"

"We have been having this fight for twenty years," Michaelis said. "I'm not having it again today. Pick me out something nice to take to a dinner, I have to impress someone."

Hugo sniffed, but handed him a bottle. "This one is fine. It wasn't meant to be aged, but aging won't have made it worse."

"And it's a nice rosé. All right." Michaelis presented the bottle to Jes. "Please say you're impressed."

"Couldn't tell you, my knowledge of wine starts with Manischewitz and ends at Three Buck Chuck," they said.

Both men looked mystified.

"Hugo, bear in mind when selecting for Noah that he has an immature palate and so does his parent," Jes sighed. "We'll probably want to sell most of what we get."

"Of course," Hugo bowed. "Your Grace?"

"You know my taste," Michaelis said. "I need to get ready for dinner. I'll see you upstairs," he said, cupping Jes's elbow briefly and heading for the door, wine still in one hand.

Hugo watched him go, then turned to Jes and offered them a bottle.

"Red is much better," he said. Jes took the bottle, nodding.

"I will bear that in mind," they said gravely.

Lachlan and Stephen's baby daughter, Bonnie, was clearly the star attendee at dinner, even though it included both Lachlan's business partner and the former king of the country.

Michaelis understood. Bonnie was Carla's only grandchild, and she was reasonably adorable. Noah, who he would not have thought would be enthusiastic about an infant, immediately took Bonnie from Stephen's arms and held her throughout dinner, feeding her spoonfuls of puree.

"He likes to be an uncle," Jes said to Michaelis after dinner, when they saw him watching Noah with perplexity. "He's had aunties and uncles and zazas his whole life. He finally gets to be older and wiser than someone."

"Ah," Michaelis nodded. "Well, Bonnie doesn't lack for support, that's for sure."

"She's one of the reasons we considered coming back," Jes said. "Lachlan and I met in New York a long time ago. He moved here to be with Stephen, and when he and Stephen adopted Bonnie he said '*something something family*, time to come home'," they said drily.

"I hope you're at least a little glad you did."

"I am," they said, sipping the wine Hugo had sent. They shot him a smile. "Didn't expect it to turn out quite this way, but I can't object. Carla," they added, in a slightly louder voice. "Did I tell you about the second time I met His Grace?"

"This sounds like it's going to be embarrassing," Carla said, folding her hands under her chin. "Sure you don't want to save it for your tell-all book, Jes?"

"Not embarrassing, just funny," Jes said, nudging Michaelis with an elbow. "The first time we met I told him midlife crises usually involve shiny cars, not podcasts. The second time, he pulls up to the studio in a classic green Jaguar."

"Which you called a Hot Wheels toy," he said.

"Honey, it looks like a Hot Wheels toy. Those things don't look real," Lachlan said.

"He rolls up in this Hot Wheels like that's going to impress us," Jes continued.

"I wasn't trying to impress anyone," Michaelis protested. "I just thought it was funny. I told you I already had a shiny car."

"He did look very heroic, soaking wet and trying to help rescue the tech," Lachlan said.

"You weren't even there," Michaelis pointed out.

"Noah sent me so many photos," Lachlan said. "When Jes writes the tell-all book there's going to be one of those old fashioned middle sections that's just photographs of you looking bedraggled."

Michaelis sat back, gesturing at his still-bruised face in resignation. "My lot in life these days."

"Isn't it more interesting, though?" Stephen asked. He was much quieter than Lachlan, but when he did speak he generally had very keen things to say, Michaelis was noticing. "I mean, as king, when was the last time you literally fished someone out of a pit?"

"Used to wish I could cast a few people into them," Michaelis remarked. "Very politically expedient, your average pit."

"Well, the wine's good, anyway," Carla said, drinking the last of hers. "And I'll be the envy of all the old biddies around here tomorrow for hosting the King Emeritus. But I'm afraid now I'm going to kick you all out except Noah, because he's going to stay up with me watching awful old horror movies."

"Don't give yourself nightmares," Jes said, kissing Noah's forehead as they rose to go. "Remember, text me tomorrow so I know you're still alive, and be home by dinner."

The evening was fine, still warm even well after sunset. Lachlan and Stephen were off to go for a drive down the coast with Bonnie; Michaelis and Jes declined the offer of a ride back and walked instead. The palace, rising up on their left, was ablaze with light.

"Gregory's entertaining the MPs. I think it's his favorite part – not hosting Parliament, but the evening entertainment in the summer," Michaelis said. "He loved those parties as a boy. The last few years of the reign I fell out of the habit. Nice to see it back."

"I suppose Eddie does the catering?"

"Do you know, I haven't asked? Since you arrived, I've been too busy to attend. I'd say we should go, but aside from a few of the juniors it's not the most scintillating conversation," Michaelis said.

"I sort of like that I've been a distraction," Jes said, as they turned off the main road of town and up the footpath, which forked left towards the palace or right towards the lodge. They pushed open the little unlocked gate that said NO ACCESS AFTER SUNSET and held it for him to pass through.

"I certainly haven't minded," he agreed. "It feels nice to have purpose again. And the company doesn't hurt."

Jes smiled. "You know, half my New York friends don't believe I know a royal. Generally the ones who knew me when I was twenty and really punk and more than a little messed up."

"You seem to have come through all right."

"Took some time. Everyone needs time to grow up, though," they said, and he let his fingers drift out to catch their hand, squeezing it. They held on and walked a little closer. "Well. Maybe you didn't."

"Depends on how you look at it. In one light, my destiny was set by the time I was twenty-two," he said. "But when you lock yourself into a path that young, once the path ends..." he shrugged. "I had a great marriage. I had a great reign, too. Wasn't ready for what came after. So I got at sixty what you got out of the way at twenty."

"Are you saying you're a little messed up?" they asked, teasing.

"Who's to say? I suppose it's a warning you may need to be patient with me."

"Michaelis," they said, stopping, and he turned and stopped as well. "If I didn't know that you required patience by now…"

He opened his mouth, a little offended, and before he could retort they broke down in laughter.

"The look on your face!" they hooted. "Oh no, can't tell the king he's sometimes difficult!"

He grinned. "All right, fine. But to be fair, I always fix my mistakes."

"You haven't gone back and fixed that one reference you got wrong in episode two."

"I did not get that reference wrong," he said, pulling them closer, "and I am going to win the fight with my detractors who are slandering my scholarship. I have citations."

"Save your citations for the show notes," they said. They looked past him, towards the lodge, lit only with a single lantern hanging from the eaves over the front door. "Would you like to come back to mine tonight?"

He considered them, a little cautious. "Are you sure?"

"If you want to wait, I don't mind," Jes said. "But if you can't see a reason to, I can't."

He glanced back over his shoulder. "I'm not looking for reasons, no. Although it did occur to me I have no idea if I'm any good in bed."

Jes laughed and leaned against him, forehead resting in the hollow of his throat. "Are you kidding me?"

"I was with one person most of my life. I might be terrible at this," he said, which only made Jes laugh harder. "Mocked, all I get is mocked. I was king!"

Jes propped their chin against his chest. "Quitter."

Michaelis raised his hands to cup their face and kissed them. "Not in this. Come on."

"We could give you a few shots of Davzda if that would help," Jes teased, as they kept walking. "Noah's a liquor magnate now, we can raid his stash."

"You have the worst ideas," he said, but on the porch of the lodge he pulled them in close again, arm around their waist. "Some other night, perhaps. I want to remember tonight."

"Good," they said with a smile, and pushed the door open. "Me too."

EPILOGUE

MICHAELIS CAME OUT of the recording studio, one afternoon in late spring, to find a flotilla of teenagers clustered around the big conference table in what used to be the bunker's war room.

"I understand we've been invaded by sea," he said, faced with a gaggle of youths in navy-blue polo shirts, brick-colored yachting shorts, and boat shoes.

"Hi, Michaelis," Noah called, slightly louder over a desynchronized chorus of children murmuring *Your Grace* shyly. "Study group."

"It will definitely take study if you want to defeat the Spanish Armada," Michaelis agreed. "Have you seen Jes?"

"They fled ahead of the invasion," one of the kids said boldly. Michaelis pointed at them.

"Amani," he said. They beamed at having been recognized. "Good to see you again. Which direction did they go?"

A couple of hands pointed up.

"Yes, I...assumed that," he said.

"Boss said they were going out on the lake," Noah said. "They asked if you'd stick around for another ten minutes until everyone had to go."

"Ah. Conscription. Carry on, then. Will anyone need a ride home?"

"No, we're gonna walk down into town, people will get rides from there."

Michaelis nodded, duty mostly discharged, and took up a strategic position in the corner, far enough away that he wouldn't be obtrusive. He reviewed the following day's calendar and paged through a script Jes had sent him for editing until the children began trickling out. Noah, last to leave, waved at Michaelis and said, "Dismissed, ensign," and Michaelis nodded.

Upstairs, he changed into a swimsuit and ambled down to the dock, walking to the end. Jes was in the boat, well out in the middle of the lake, with what looked like a cooler. He stepped out of his shoes and dove in, enjoying the brief, brisk swim out to the boat. By the time he reached them, they were sitting up, arms on their knees, a skeptical look on their face.

"If you capsize me, I'll end you," they said.

"How long do you think I've been doing this?" he asked, hefting himself into the boat without even rocking it that much. It did require an undignified tumble onto his back, but from there he could dangle one leg out of the boat and look up at them upside-down, which he knew charmed them.

"All the kids gone? The noise was starting to get to me and I figured they couldn't get into too much trouble," they said.

"Yep. Nice to see Noah with so many friends." He sat up and shook water out of his hair, sliding around so that he fell into their lap backwards, head on their chest, arms resting on their knees. "Bliss."

"Closest I've found," Jes agreed. "Beer and snacks in the cooler if you want something."

"No, I'm fine. Are you comfortable?" he asked.

"Yep." One of their hands rested over his heart, and he felt a kiss dropped into his hair. "Can I run something past you?"

"Of course."

They propped their phone on his chest, open to an image of a person in a tuxedo that flowed into a dramatic, elegant ball gown in the lower half.

"Couldn't pull that off, not with my hips," he said.

"Don't sell yourself short. This is option one. Option two," they said, and flicked to the next image, which showed a vivid orange sheath dress, rather traditional for their usual tastes, shot through with gold. "And option three…"

The third outfit was a midnight-blue men's suit with velvet lapels. The model wore a shimmering blouse under the suit jacket, with a banded collar and a cutout below it, deep to show decolletage. He whistled low.

"These are for the coronation anniversary ball?" he asked.

"Considering my options. I'd like to stun, but subtly."

"You'd look fine in any of them, but you could have something made. Or buy a couple, pick out what you want on the day. Won't be the last formal you have to attend, probably. I'll be in the uniform, so it's easy to coordinate with anything you wear."

"I'm thinking option three," Jes said contemplatively.

"I like it, but you don't normally do cleavage."

"True. I don't know, it seemed like somewhere I'd like to go a little femme. Would you mind?"

"Not in the least, you know that." He turned his head to look up at them, nose bumping their collarbone. "We aren't being presented to court. Eddie has to follow the rules, for once in his life. You never have to, Caez."

"Too late for Caez. I'm relegated to Consort of the King Emeritus."

"Caez of my heart," he said. They scruffed his hair gently.

"All right, I'll make a decision tonight," they said. "I was going to stay out here another hour or so."

"Perfect. Mind if I sleep?"

"Keeps you out of mischief," Jes said. Michaelis settled in, eyes closing, and didn't even startle when he felt their arm drape over his shoulder and their palm drift down his abdomen, fingertips tracing gently across the skin.

"I love that," he said drowsily, and felt Jes smile against the crown of his head.

"What, belly rubs?" they asked, amused. He shifted a little, eyes slitting open.

"I love the touch," he said, pleased with how easy the words came. Sometimes they didn't, but he was working on it. "And I love that it's you doing it."

"I'm glad," they said. "I love you too."

"Hm." He closed his eyes again. "Wake me when you get bored."

"Sleep a while. We have plenty of time," Jes assured him.

He heard, distantly, a beep, and then the soft chatter of voices. He fell asleep to Jes's breathing and the low murmur of their headphones as they caught up on the day's listening.

THE REVERB PODCAST NETWORK
ASKAZER-SHIVADLAKIA OFFICE

Jes Deimos:
Executive Producer, CEO
Host, *The Echo*
Host, *All On Mike*

Lachlan Hines:
Executive Producer, COO
Producer, *The Echo*
Producer, *The Echo Junior*
Host and Producer, *How To Make Some Noise*
Producer, *All On Mike*

Noah Deimos:
Junior Producer, Staff
Host, *The Echo Junior*
Host, *How To Make Some Noise*
Host and Producer, *Being On Boats*

Michaelis ben Jason:
Partner Producer
Host, *All On Mike*
Host, *How To Make Some Noise*
Host and Producer, *The Royal Reads*

CONTENT WARNINGS:

This listing is to the best of my ability and made in good faith.

- Brief mentions of spousal death and grieving (throughout book). Michaelis is still grieving his wife, who passed several years before, and processing the grief throughout the story.
- Brief discussion of family-related trauma (Chapter 4). Noah speaks with Michaelis about Jes's relationship with their parents; this <u>does not</u> involve transphobia regarding Jes's gender, just their parents being run of the mill assholes.
- Extensive discussion of alcohol and drinking (Chapter 5; some discussion of hangovers etc. in Chapter 6). Jes and Michaelis play a drinking game where Michaelis becomes progressively more intoxicated. No trauma or negative consequences result.
- Mention of injuries and description of wounds and blood (Chapter 9). Nothing graphic; Michaelis receives scrapes and cuts that bleed somewhat before being treated.
- Child briefly endangered (Chapter 9). Noah ends up trapped underground by an accident and must be rescued; no permanent harm or trauma.